96/7

D0373009

8

# A DIXIE MORRIS ANIMAL ADVENTURE

DIXIE

*To Uncle Buddy,*
*my favorite soldier.*
*I love you very much.*
*Dixie*

# CONTENTS

**D**ixie Morris moved slowly along the bank of CDs that filled the counter. She stuck her tongue out one corner of her mouth and thought hard.

She held one in each hand and wished she had money to buy both.

Suddenly a voice sounded behind her. "Hey, Dix, what you doing? Weighing them?"

Dixie jumped and whirled around. "Manny Romanos, what do you mean sneaking up on me like that?"

"I didn't sneak!"

Manny Romanos was eleven, exactly Dixie's age. He was a gypsy boy and one of Dixie's best friends.

He grinned. "You need some help?"

"No, I don't!" Dixie snapped. "I can pick out my own CDs!" She put down both

CDs and picked up another. "This is a good one. I'm going to buy it."

She paid for the CD, and Manny walked with her out of the store.

It was cold outside, for fall was on the way. Dixie pulled her green sweater closer around her and shivered a little.

"Are you coming over to practice today?" he asked. "You've missed the last four days."

"I know. I've been real busy," Dixie said. "How's Champ?"

"He's fine."

Champ. The Romanoses' fine horse. Dixie had learned to ride the barrels on Champ. She had learned so well that she'd beaten her arch rival, Francine Mosely, at the rodeo.

They walked along Main Street, saying hi to people. Then Manny said, "Let's go get some ice cream."

"I don't have much money."

"I've got some." He led the way to Baskin Robbins, where he swept his hand in a gesture indicating all the flavors listed. "Anything you want."

"You mean—*anything*?"

"Sure," Manny said grandly. "I've got the money."

"Then let's share a banana split."

"All right."

The girl behind the counter was a senior in high school.

Dixie said, "Agnes, we want chocolate, strawberry, and vanilla. With butterscotch, chocolate, and strawberry topping. And marshmallows. And cover it up with nuts until you can't even see it."

Agnes grinned at Dixie and winked at her. "That's the way. When you got a man, make 'em pay!"

When Agnes came with their ice cream, Manny paid and put the change in his pocket. "Let's sit over there by the window—where we can watch people go by."

They were halfway through the banana split when a tall young man with straw-colored hair and a pair of striking blue eyes came in. He was wearing blue jeans and a sweatshirt that said "University of Arkansas" on it. "Hi, guys. How you doing?"

"Great, Hank," Dixie said. "Manny's treating today. You'd better get in on it."

"That's right, preacher," Manny said, "anything you'd like."

Hank Williams, the youth pastor at the local church, said, "Well, I'll just have a sin-

9

gle dip of vanilla. And I'll pay for it myself."

"Is that all?" Manny snorted. "Man, you don't know how to live! Go on, have two dips. Tell Agnes to put it on my bill."

Hank Williams allowed Manny to pay for his ice cream, but probably made a mental note to make it up to him in the future. He took a chair at the table and soon was nibbling at his vanilla ice cream.

"So what's up, preacher?" Manny asked.

Hank Williams paused in his eating to say, "I just heard big news. The church has approved our young people going on a mission trip next summer."

"No fooling?" Dixie asked, interested at once. "Where are you going?"

"We're going to Belize."

"I thought they'd be going somewhere here in the States," she said. "Where is *Belize?*"

Hank Williams took another swipe at his ice cream. "You go to Mexico and turn left."

"I know where Belize is," Manny said. "It's a little country off the coast next to Guatemala."

"How'd you know *that?*" the youth pastor asked.

"I like maps. I look at them all the time. That's where it is, isn't it?"

"That's right. A little country about fifty miles wide and maybe a hundred and fifty to two hundred miles long. About the size of Israel. Or Taiwan."

"What do you do on a trip like that?" Manny asked.

"We'll visit different churches and help them tell people about Jesus. So we'll need to plan a program—singing, maybe puppets, giving our testimonies. Some groups help by putting up a church building."

"Ooh, that would be fun!" Dixie said.

"But the *reason* for a missions trip is not to have fun. We're there to help. Some of it might be fun, but it also can mean pretty rough living. On my last trip I had to sleep on a concrete floor."

"I wouldn't mind," Manny said. "We Romanies are tough! Not sissies like you folks!"

"That's what you think!" Dixie said. "I can rough it just as good as you can!" She turned back to the youth pastor. "I want to go, Pastor Hank! Do you think I'm old enough?"

"Well, you're right on the borderline,

Dixie. I sort of made a rule in my head that you have to be at least twelve."

"I'm *almost* twelve!" Dixie insisted.

"So am I!" Manny said. "I could help you do stuff."

"Well—" Pastor Hank stroked his chin "—I would have to break my own rule. And you'd need approval by both the church and your parents. And, of course, it's going to cost money."

"How much money?" Manny asked.

"You'd have to have at least five hundred dollars."

"Five hundred dollars!" both Dixie and Manny exclaimed.

"I haven't got five hundred dollars!" Dixie said.

"Neither do I," Manny echoed.

"If God wants you to go, He'll provide the money. I doubt if *any* of our young people have five hundred dollars right now. But if you want to be a part of the team, kids, you'll have to start in right now. I'd suggest you begin with the permissions."

They sat at the table awhile, talking about Belize, and the jungle, and the Indians, and the trip down. The more they talked, the more excited Dixie and Manny grew.

Then Hank Williams got up. "I've got to go now. Talk to your folks about what you'd like to do."

"We will," Dixie agreed. "I think Aunt Edith and Uncle Roy will let me go if I can raise the money somehow."

When Pastor Hank was gone, Dixie said to Manny. "I'm going to go!"

"Five hundred dollars is a lot of money!"

"But it's like he said—God can provide it. God owns everything."

Manny rubbed his fingers through his thick black hair. "God will have to do it. My folks sure don't have that kind of money."

Candy Sweet, Uncle Roy and Aunt Edith's hired hand, was waiting in the pickup to take them home. Dixie was staying with this aunt and uncle while her parents built a house for the family in Africa, where they were missionaries.

"You all about ready?" Candy asked. He was a big man with fair hair and mild blue eyes. He spoke very slowly.

"We're ready," Dixie said, and she and Manny piled into the truck.

The Romanoses lived three miles past the Snyder farm, and Candy took Manny home first.

When Manny got out, he said, "Come over and do your riding, Dixie. We've got to practice for that rodeo over at Fairhope."

"I will. And don't forget to start praying for our five hundred dollars apiece."

As Candy turned the truck around and headed for home, he said, "What's this about five hundred dollars? For the *rodeo?*"

"Oh, no. The church is sending a bunch of kids to Belize . . ." Dixie rambled on about wanting to go.

All Candy said was, "Five hundred dollars is a lot of money."

"Sure is." Dixie gave him a worried look. "And I don't know where I'm going to get it."

Aunt Edith was a thin, nervous woman with gray hair and glasses. She had been ill but was doing much better now. She met Dixie at the door with some letters.

"Dixie, you got a letter from your Aunt Sarah and from your parents, too."

"Oh, goody!"

She opened the one from her mom and dad first. She read it quickly and then handed it to her aunt. "The house is going

14

to be finished pretty soon, and I can go live with them. We'll all be together again!"

Then she tore open the other letter, read the first few lines, and cried, "Listen to this! Aunt Sarah is leaving the circus!"

"I didn't think she'd ever do that."

Sarah Logan was Dixie's young aunt. She was a veterinarian for a traveling circus, and Dixie had lived with her awhile. She still missed her circus friends and all the animals.

"She's coming *here!*" Dixie exclaimed next. "She's going to open a veterinarian practice right here in Milo."

"Well, isn't that fine!" Aunt Edith beamed. "Now we'll have a vet again. We haven't had one since Dr. Thomas moved away."

Dixie ran to her room and quickly changed clothes. Then she sat on the bed and read her letters again. She was happy that she would be going to Africa soon, but she was also happy that Aunt Sarah was coming to Milo.

"Boy, Aunt Sarah, you'll have a lot to do around here, and we'll have a good time together!"

## 2
# THE NEW FAMILY

**D**ixie crawled out of bed, as tired as if she had been up all night. She had lain awake, thinking about what it would be like to live in Africa. She wondered if she would see lions and elephants close to where she would live. Then her thoughts turned to Aunt Sarah. She was excited about her aunt's coming here, for they were the best of friends.

She picked out her oldest pair of blue jeans and a pale blue T-shirt. Then she showered, washed her hair, and dried it. All the time, she was thinking about the things that were going to happen.

*But where am I going to get five hundred dollars?*

That thought sat in her mind as she brushed her long blonde hair—and that took a while. By the time she tied it in a ponytail and went down to start breakfast, she was no closer to having an answer than when she'd started brushing.

Cooking was one thing Dixie had found that she could do well. She decided to fix an extrabig breakfast for everyone this morning.

She started with pancakes. She loved pancakes, and she knew that Candy liked them better than anything else.

For her uncle and aunt she made omelets with lots of cheese. Then she popped toast into the toaster and made it a golden brown. By the time breakfast was ready, Candy had come in from his little cabin, and her aunt and uncle had arrived.

"What a big breakfast!" Uncle Roy exclaimed happily. "If you keep feeding me like this, I'm going to be fat and pretty."

"You're already fat and pretty, Uncle Roy." Dixie liked her uncle very much. He was a big man with a face burned from the sun and a head that was balding on top. He had kind brown eyes, and she knew he would do anything for her.

Candy said only, "It all looks good to me."

"What are you going to do with your Saturday, Dixie?" Aunt Edith asked as they ate.

"I'm going over and practice riding Champ."

"I hear Francine Mosely's telling around that she's going to beat you at the next rodeo," Uncle Roy said. He winked at her. "Don't you let her do it. No matter if she has got a horse that cost a million dollars."

"Oh, he didn't cost a million, but he is a fine horse. No better than Champ, though," Dixie added loyally.

When breakfast was over, Aunt Edith said, "You go ahead, Dixie. I'll clean up this morning. And the breakfast was wonderful."

"Sure was," Uncle Roy said. "I could eat another one right now."

Candy smiled shyly. "I could eat another one in about an hour, I reckon. But this will have to do for now. Real good, Dixie. You want me to give you a ride down to the Romanos place in the truck?"

"No, I'll just ride my bike. That way you won't have to come after me."

Dixie grabbed a sweater, pulled a toboggan cap over her ears, and dashed out the front door. She jumped on her bike and pedaled out of the yard at full speed. It had rained the day before, and she dodged between the puddles. Even so, she splattered mud all over her Doc Marten boots. Some ducks were crossing the road on their way to the pond—she ran through them, laughing at their angry squawks.

White fleecy clouds drifted across the dark blue sky. It was like a summer day except that it was colder.

When she rolled into the Romanos yard, Manny came out of the barn and leaped across a fence to greet her. "I stayed up all night thinking of a way to get five hundred dollars. I'd have to rob a bank!" he exclaimed.

"Don't talk like that, Manny!"

"Just kidding. But I can't think of any other way."

"I can't either, but I'm not going to worry about it. God's going to take care of it."

"Can you stay all day?"

"I have to go home at noon. I've got some chores to do."

"Well, let's see if you've forgotten how to saddle a horse."

Dixie had not forgotten. As she saddled Champ, he playfully nipped at her hair. She slapped him gently on the nose. "You stop that! Save all that energy for your running."

Expertly she put on the bridle. Then she mounted the beautiful horse in one smooth motion. Champ pranced around a little, and Dixie let him have his fun. Then she said, "Now let's see what you can do."

She directed Champ into the large pasture where three barrels stood in a cloverleaf pattern. She focused on the first barrel as Manny pulled out a stopwatch.

"Get a good run at it, and let's see what you can do!" he said.

Dixie kicked Champ with her heels, hollering, "Go for it, Champ!"

The horse shot toward barrel number one. Dixie leaned forward to keep her balance and kept her eyes on the first barrel.

"Got it!" she heard her timer yell as she passed where he stood.

The object of barrel racing was to take the horse around the barrels as fast as possible. She rounded the first one, leaning to the side as Champ leaned toward the barrel. He was a smart horse and knew exactly what to do.

They drove toward the second barrel. Champ's muscles propelled him across the distance as though he'd been shot out of a gun. Once again Dixie leaned into the turn. When they came out of it, she yelled, "One more, Champ! Go!"

Champ approached number three, and they went into the turn. But this time her toe struck the barrel, and over it went.

She went on to finish the turn even though she knew, if it had been a real contest, that she wouldn't win. Manny had told her, "Never stop. Not even if you knock down all three barrels."

She sailed by where Manny stood with the stopwatch, then pulled up Champ and patted him on the shoulder. "Good run, Champ."

"Not bad. Seventeen seconds," Manny said.

"The barrel was my fault. My foot hit it."

Manny grinned. "Judges don't ask. If a barrel goes down, it's down—no matter if the wind blows it over."

They practiced off and on all morning, taking time out to let Champ rest. They even went down to the pond, fished awhile, and came back with a string of perch.

Mr. Romanos came outside and watched them cleaning the fish. He had the same black hair and dark eyes as his son. He held his fiddle in his hand. "How did it go today?"

"Went great, Dad," Manny said. "I couldn't have done it better myself."

Dixie knew that Manny was teasing her. "I'll just let you try it sometime," she said. "Here, clean the rest of these fish. I'm going to play with Emily."

She spent the next half hour with the dark-haired two year old, while Rolf and Sonia, the other two Romanos children, watched.

Manny's pretty mother said, "I'm glad to hear you're doing so well with the riding."

"Manny thinks we'll win."

"Manny always thinks he'll win," Sonia said.

By noon, clouds were coming up. Dixie said, "I'd better be getting home. It looks like it might rain."

"Getting colder too." Manny shivered and pulled the front of his leather jacket closer together. "See you at school tomorrow."

"OK. It was fun, Manny."

Before Dixie had gone a half mile, dark clouds were rolling over. She pedaled as hard as she could.

When she came to the creek, she thought, *I'd better be careful here.* It was a small creek, but it had several deep spots in it. Dixie had crossed it before, though. *I'll just go real fast,* she thought.

Her plan would have worked except for one thing. When she was halfway across, the front wheel dropped into a deep hole, and the front end of the bicycle disappeared. Dixie, with a cry of dismay, flew over the handlebars. She turned a complete somersault and landed on her back in the freezing water.

Dixie struggled to her feet. She saw her cap floating away and grabbed for it. The wind was whipping around her so that her teeth began to chatter.

"I never saw anybody cross a creek like that."

Dixie wheeled around. A boy about her age stood laughing at her. He was wearing tightfitting jeans, and his hair was almost as dark as Manny Romanos's. His skin was very bronze.

"It's not nice to laugh at people when they fall down!"

"Oh, I thought you did it on purpose! It looked so neat, the way you turned a somersault."

Furious, Dixie pulled on her cap. But it was soaked, and the water ran into her eyes. She groped around for the handlebars, jerked up the bicycle, and floundered out of the creek.

The boy—he was still watching her!—said, "You're gonna freeze."

"You just be quiet!" Dixie snapped.

"If you try to get home like that—wherever you live—you're gonna catch pneumonia."

"Don't worry about me."

But suddenly the boy took the handlebars away from her. "You'd better come to my house and dry out."

Dixie glared at him. "Who are you? I never saw you around here before." She was so embarrassed about making such a spectacle out of herself. But she *was* shivering, and she knew she was prone to catch cold when she got wet in chilly weather.

"I'm Jared Eagle. Me and my dad just moved into the house through those trees."

"The old Templeton place?"

"I guess so. We bought it. Just moved in yesterday. Come on, girl. You're going to freeze to death."

Dixie still hesitated, but she did feel the icy fingers of cold right down to her bones. "All right," she said. "I guess it won't hurt to dry out."

Jared pushed the bicycle. He ran rather than walked, and Dixie ran to keep up with him. They followed a twisting gravel road.

On the other side of some oaks, in an open space, sat the Templeton place. It was a small house with a steep-pitched roof. Dixie had never been inside.

When they reached the front of the house, the boy yelled, "Hey, Dad! We got company!"

The door opened, and a very tall man stepped out. He had the same black hair and dark blue eyes as his son. He was wearing a leather shirt and dark brown pants and well-worn boots.

"And who's this?" the man demanded.

"Don't know. She fell in the creek. I thought I'd better bring her here to get dried out before she died of pneumonia." He said to Dixie, "This is my dad."

Dixie was pretty sure now, from the name "Eagle" and the man's lean coppery face, that James Eagle and his son were Native Americans. She had never seen a live Native American before.

Mr. Eagle didn't say anything for a second, but finally he nodded. "Well, come on in."

It was not a gracious invitation, but by now Dixie was shaking from the cold.

She was glad to see a glowing fireplace at one end of the large room.

"Go on over there and dry out," Mr. Eagle said. Jared Eagle's father seemed rather irritated by everything.

But Dixie knew she had to dry out. She stood beside the fire, and the heat felt wonderful.

"I appreciate your help," she said to Jared, who kept watching her. "I probably would have frozen before I got home. I live three miles down the road. My name's Dixie Morris. I live with my uncle and aunt—the Snyders . . ."

They listened, but neither spoke, and Dixie was embarrassed at having to do all the talking. Then she heard a sound that she had not expected. She looked quickly at Mr. Eagle. "Is that a *baby?*"

"Of course, it's a baby," the man said. "Didn't you ever hear a baby cry before?"

"Sure," Dixie said, "but I didn't see him, or is it a her?"

"It's a her," Jared said. "It's my little sister."

James Eagle crossed the room and picked up a bundle from a wooden cradle. He held the bundle, looked down at it, and the severe look on his face softened. "I guess you're hungry, and maybe you need a change too."

"I'll fix the baby food if you'll do the changing, Dad."

"OK, Jared. That sounds like a bargain."

Dixie toasted herself on one side, then on the other, from time to time watching the boy.

He went to the kitchen area at the far end of the room and opened a can. "Won't take but a minute, Dad," he said. "How you coming?"

The big man placed the baby on a couch. It was obvious that he was not very good at changing diapers. He mumbled, "I'll be glad when you get big enough to wear grown-up clothes."

"How old is the baby?"

"Not quite a year."

Dixie said before she thought, "Your wife's not here?"

Both the man and the boy looked at her. Dixie knew she had said something wrong, but she could not think what.

Then Jared muttered, "My mom died when Dreama was born."

"Oh, I'm so sorry!" Dixie was horrified. She tried to say something else. "Is that her name—Dreama? It's pretty. I never heard of a name like that before."

"That's what my wife named her."

Dixie turned back to the fireplace. The man and the boy were obviously still grieving. She did not know how to say anything to make it any better. She took off her shoes, wrung out her socks, and put them on a rack where some diapers were hanging. Then for a long time she just quietly stood, steaming and drying out.

By this time the baby had been fed. Dixie said timidly, "Could I hold her?"

"I suppose so." Mr. Eagle deposited the baby in Dixie's arms.

Dixie said, "She's beautiful! What pretty hair she has. It's not as black as yours, Mr. Eagle."

"No, her mother had red hair."

"She sure is a pretty baby." Dixie began to touch the baby's cheek with a finger. "Look, she's smiling at me!"

"She's a pretty happy baby," Jared said. He sat on a stool and watched as Dixie played with the baby.

His father suddenly walked out of the room.

Jared broke the silence finally. "I don't guess you've ever known any Indians."

"I know that some people like you like to be called Native Americans instead of Indians."

"I don't care," Jared said. "What difference does it make? My dad—he's half white himself. And Mom was half white, so that makes me . . . I never could figure it out."

Dixie said thoughtfully, "We've been studying about Indians. Our book says that some of the Indians were treated badly."

"That was a long time ago," Jared said.

"I guess it was."

"You can't change the past. Just as long

as people treat us OK *now,* that's all I care about."

Dixie held the baby for so long that she suddenly said, "Oops, I think she needs to be changed again."

Jared groaned. "I can't do that too good."

"I haven't had much practice," Dixie said, "but let me try."

Jared eagerly accepted her offer. "Here's the diapers up on this rack."

Dixie's friend Martha Ingalls had a baby sister, and Dixie had watched Martha change the baby. She had even changed the Ingalls baby a few times herself. She did Dreama's diaper change quickly and efficiently.

Jared had been watching her. "How'd you do that so quick?"

Mr. Eagle walked in at that moment.

"Look, Dad. Look how good she fixed the diaper on Dreama."

Mr. Eagle strolled to the couch. Surprise came over his fine-looking face. "I guess it takes a woman's touch," he said.

"Jared, how old are you?" Dixie asked suddenly.

"Eleven."

"Good. I'm eleven, too. We'll be in the same classes at school."

Jared gave his father a quick look. "I don't see why I have to go to school."

"We've been over that, Jared," his father said. "Let's not argue about it any-more. Now at least you know somebody." He smiled at Dixie for the first time. Perfect white teeth gleamed against his dark skin.

"My folks will be glad to meet you, too."

"Your folks are named Snyder?" Mr. Eagle asked.

"That's my uncle and aunt. My real par-ents are named Morris. They're in Africa."

"What are they doing in *Africa?*" Jared exclaimed.

"They're missionaries. I'm going to go be with them as soon as they get a house built for us all to live in."

"Wow, you mean right in the middle of the lions and the tigers?"

"There aren't any tigers in Africa. They're in India and other places," Dixie informed him. "Well, I'm just about dry. I'd better get home. It still looks like rain. See you in school tomorrow, Jared." She turned to the man. "I'm glad to meet you, Mr. Eagle. I hope you and Jared can come to church Sunday."

An odd expression crossed the man's face. "We don't go to church," he said gruffly.

"Oh!" Dixie said, knowing that a door had been slammed in her face. "Well, anyway, we're glad to have some new neighbors. Jared, I'll see you in school."

On her way home Dixie wondered about the new family. "It's kind of sad," she said out loud. "You can tell they really miss Mrs. Eagle." It was sad to think that they had to get along without her.

"I'll just do the best I can to make Jared feel at home. And Mr. Eagle too. I'll ask Pastor Stone to come by and visit them. Maybe *he* can get them to come to church."

# 3

# A TRIP TO BELIZE

**A**unt Sarah!"

Dixie ran as fast as she could and threw her arms around the woman who had just gotten out of the fiery red Jeep Cherokee.

"Be careful—you'll hurt an old lady!" Sarah Logan was young and pretty with brilliant red hair and green eyes. She had on worn jeans, a white T-shirt, and black half boots. She hugged Dixie hard, stepped back and took her by the shoulders.

"My, you've grown, Dixie!"

"Oh, Aunt Sarah, it's so good to see you again! I've missed you so much."

"I've missed you, too, Dixie. And I brought letters from all your circus friends." Her aunt reached into the Jeep for her purse and pulled out a bundle of letters with a rubber band around them. "You'll be kept busy answering these, I think."

Dixie took the letters in one hand and grabbed Sarah's hand with the other. "Come on inside. I'll bet you're hungry. I'm going to fix lunch for you, all by myself."

Sarah Logan allowed herself to be pulled into the house, where she was greeted by the Snyders. Thirty minutes later, after she had been installed in the guest room, she was back in the kitchen.

"This is a lunch big enough for circus roustabouts!" she exclaimed, looking over the plate of eggs, another of bacon, and still a third of fat, golden-brown biscuits. "I've missed your good cooking, Dixie."

"Well, you won't have to miss it anymore. You're going to stay with us."

"Oh, I'm not expecting to do that!" Sarah said, sitting down. "It would be too big an inconvenience for you."

"Don't talk foolish!" Uncle Roy snorted. "We could always use a doctor around the place."

"But I'm a *veterinarian.*"

"I've never seen much difference." Uncle Roy grinned. "When something alive gets sick, it needs doctoring, whether it's a horse, or a raccoon, or a human being."

They all bowed their heads, and Aunt Sarah said a quick prayer. Then, while she ate, she listened to Dixie talk excitedly about all the things she had been doing. Dixie had not gone far into her list of activities before she mentioned the Eagles.

"Who are the Eagles?"

"It's a family that just moved in," Dixie said. "Way back in the woods. It's hard to get to." Then she said, "They're Indians. Part Indian, anyway. And I feel so sorry for them."

"Because they're Indians?"

"No. Because Mrs. Eagle died and left a little baby. Her name is Dreama, and she's not a year old yet, and those two just don't know how to take care of her."

"What two?"

"Her father—Mr. Eagle—and his son is Jared."

"How old is Jared?"

"Eleven, the same as I am."

Sarah took a bite of biscuit, then smiled. "Well, I'll be glad to meet them. But first I've got to get my office set up."

"You have a place in mind?" Uncle Roy asked.

"Not yet, but there ought to be *something* available in town."

"I'll go along and help you look, Aunt Sarah. We're out of school today. There's a teachers' meeting."

"That'll be fine. Just let me finish lunch here, and we'll see what we can find."

The rest of the day was a whirlwind. Aunt Sarah and Dixie looked at every place in Milo that might possibly be used for a veterinarian's office. Finding a suitable place was extra difficult because Aunt Sarah had to have an outdoor section to use as a run for some of the animals.

Finally they encountered Sheriff Henry Peck. He smiled broadly when he saw Aunt Sarah. "Well, now, Sarah," he said. "Glad to have you back. Ever since Doc Wilson left six months ago, we haven't had a vet. Right now one of my Walker hounds needs looking at."

"I'll come by after we find a place for an office." Sarah sighed wearily. "But so far we haven't found one."

"You need a place to set up? I know of something that just might interest you," Sheriff Peck said. "A fellow started a store out on the edge of town. It sits on about two acres, mostly woods. It's kind of run-down, because the store didn't make it, but I think it might do."

"Who owns it, Sheriff?"

"I think the bank took it over, and I expect they'd be glad to rent it to you. Want me to go and get the key from Mr. Olaf down at the bank?"

"Would you do that?"

"Sure!" Sheriff Peck grinned again. "No serious crime going on at the moment."

They all went to the bank, where the sheriff picked up the key. Then they got back into the Jeep, and he had Sarah head north a short way on Highway 20.

"There it is!" he said. "Right over there on the left. See?"

"Oh, that looks very nice! It's got big trees around it. I like that."

"As I said, the inside is probably in pretty bad shape. The fellow that owned it left in a hurry, and then some vandals got in. But if it'll do, I think the price would be right."

Aunt Sarah stopped the Jeep in front of the abandoned store. They got out and walked up onto the porch.

"This is nice and close to town," Dixie said.

Sheriff Peck unlocked the door, and they stepped inside.

The place was indeed a mess. Some of the kitchen shelves still had remnants of groceries on them. A sack of flour had been broken open. Some food was scattered over the floor.

Sheriff Peck grunted. "It'll take a powerful sight of cleaning to get this place in shape."

But Dixie saw that her aunt's eyes were sparkling.

"Let's see what's in the back," Aunt Sarah said.

When they went through a rear door and found another large room, she said, "This is big enough to put cages in here." And by the time they returned to the Jeep, she had made up her mind. "This will do fine. I'll have to work hard to get it cleaned up, but it will be fine."

"You can hire some help for the clean-up. Get some of these kids to do it. Mine, for example. They need to learn what hard work is like."

Back in town, Aunt Sarah went by the

bank and arranged to rent the old store. Dixie sat listening while the business arrangements were made. When they left, Dixie said, "I'll tell all my friends, Aunt Sarah. We'll clean up the place for you."

"That'll certainly help, Dixie. Thank you. We'll hire somebody to do the heavy work."

They told the sheriff good-bye and started toward the Snyder farm.

The sun was just going down, and Dixie was admiring the sunset when a thought occurred to her.

"Aunt Sarah, I've got to have some money."

"Don't we all?" Aunt Sarah grinned. "And what do you especially need money for?"

"The church is going to send the youth group on a mission trip, but we have to pay our own way. It'll take about five hundred dollars for me to go."

"That's a lot of money. I wish I had it to give to you. But I'll be about broke by the time I get my office fixed up."

"Oh, you don't have to do that! I've decided to ask God for it—if He wants me to go."

"You always did believe in asking God for things." Sarah smiled. "I'll pray with you about it, sweetheart."

"Good! Now, about getting your office all fixed . . ."

Dixie looked around Aunt Sarah's waiting room. She was pleased with the new tile, the fresh buff paint on the walls, and the efficient-looking desk. Her aunt had hired a carpenter to create this room where people could bring their small animals. The animal clinic had been open for two weeks.

"It looks good," she said. "Maybe I can be the receptionist when I'm not in school."

"Maybe you can." Aunt Sarah was busy with records. "You've been a big help already."

"It's been fun. I'm going to give Hugo a bath now."

Hugo was a full-grown Saint Bernard.

"You'd better let me help you."

"I can do it, Aunt Sarah."

"Well, if you want to try, it'll be all right—he's very gentle. He's just so *big*."

"Hugo and I will get along fine. You'll see."

Dixie went back into the area of the building that had been set apart for dipping. First she filled the vat with water and added shampoo. Then she went outside.

A beautiful Saint Bernard got up from where he was lying in the shade of a large hickory. He came to her with his tongue lolling out. *"Wuff,"* he said.

"Hello, Hugo, are you ready for your bath?"

*"Wuff! Wuff!"*

"I guess that means yes. Well, come along, and we'll get you all nice and clean."

Hugo padded along beside her. He came almost to her chest and had massive legs.

When they reached the room where the vat was, for some reason Hugo tried to turn and go back outside. Dixie shut the door quickly. "Now, don't you be nervous, Hugo. It's going to be fun."

She had bathed several smaller dogs but never one as large as Hugo. She had taken him walking often, though. He was very obedient and would not hurt a flea. However, he seemed highly suspicious of the vat of water.

"Come on, Hugo!" Dixie grabbed the

dog by the fur around his neck and began to pull. It was like trying to pull a truck. He planted his big feet and would not move. Dixie began to plead, "Come, Hugo. It'll be fun. You'll like it."

All efforts failed, however. Finally, Dixie remembered how much Hugo liked the dog treats that Aunt Sarah kept for special occasions. She ran to a cabinet, opened a bag, and took out a handful. She held one out to the dog. "Here, Hugo. Don't you want your nice puppy biscuit?"

*"Wuff! Wuff!"* Hugo came close enough to take one of the treats.

Encouraged, Dixie backed up. "Come on, here's another one."

*"Wuff! Wuff!"*

Step by step, Dixie lured him toward the water.

The vat was no more than two feet high. Quickly she reached down and lifted one of his legs. She managed to get one foot into the vat.

But the touch of the water electrified Hugo, and he gave a mighty lunge. He only brushed against Dixie, but he weighed so much that he threw her off balance. The back of her legs hit the edge of the vat, and she fell in.

"Help!"

Water closed over her head. She struggled to get to the surface. The soapy dog shampoo was churned into foam. It got into her eyes and burned. She sat up quickly, trying to get the soap out of her eyes. She sputtered and spit out the water that had gone into her mouth.

"I've seen people give dogs a bath, but I never saw a dog give a girl a bath!"

Dixie spit out more soapy-tasting water, wiped her eyes on her sleeve, and managed to open them a slit.

Manny Romanos stood grinning at her.

"Well, don't just stand there! Help me get out!"

"Not me," Manny said. "I might fall in."

Dixie groped her way out of the vat.

Manny found a towel for her. "Here. If you're all clean, you might want to dry off now."

Dixie wiped her face. "Don't *look* at me!"

"Why not?" Manny was still grinning. He looked like the gypsy he was. He had swarthy skin, wore a bright red shirt, and had a gold earring in his right ear. "Probably the cleanest you've ever been."

Dixie knew he was teasing, but she was still embarrassed. She said, "You get away from here, Manny!"

"I thought we'd go over and practice barrel riding awhile."

"I can't go looking like this!"

"Champ wouldn't mind. He'd like you any way."

"Oh, just leave me alone!"

Dixie shoved him aside and started for the door.

The door opened, and Aunt Sarah came in. She stood still. "Dixie, what happened?"

"I think the big dog was giving her a bath, Miss Sarah," Manny said.

"I told you to go away, Manny! I don't want to talk to you!"

Manny shrugged. "If that's the way you feel about it. But if you want to practice riding, come on out this afternoon."

Dixie sniffed. "I don't know whether I will or not." She waited until Manny was gone and then turned to Aunt Sarah. "Why did I have to do a dumb thing like that?"

Aunt Sarah obviously was trying hard to keep from laughing. "It could have been worse. It's only soap and water. And you're already wet, so we might as well get that monster in the tub."

By the time Hugo was bathed and they had blown him dry with hair dryers, Dixie could laugh about it. "I guess I'm no expert at bathing Saint Bernards."

"It's hard to handle a big animal like that when they don't want to do what you want them to do."

At that moment a voice sounded outside, and Aunt Sarah looked up. "That must be another patient coming."

It was not another patient. It was Pastor Hank Williams. "Just going by," he said. Then he saw Dixie. "How'd you get so wet?"

"Don't ask," Aunt Sarah said.

But Dixie was feeling better now. "I was trying to give Hugo here a bath, and he bumped me into the tub."

Hank Williams laughed. "Now you don't have to take a shower tonight."

Dixie decided to change the subject. "How's the trip going?"

"It's going fine. I've contacted a missionary down there who's going to travel with us. He and his wife have been in Belize for a long time."

"I don't know if I'm going to get to go or not."

"Your aunt and uncle think you shouldn't go?" Hank asked.

"No, it's the money. Five hundred dollars is such a lot of money."

"It is. But God can do anything."

"I know," Dixie said. "And I'm praying."

Hank turned to Aunt Sarah. "Why don't you go along, Miss Logan? The folks down there could use a good vet."

"I might just do that, but I'd have to make the money first. I'm already helping Dixie pray for her five hundred. I'd have to pray for mine too."

Hank looked thoughtful. "It would be a life-changing experience for you both. After somebody goes to a third-world country, they never think the same again. They see poverty that they've never seen before. Some things that we take for granted, people just don't have in other places. I was in one village in Belize last year where people slept on the ground—inside huts with cracks in the walls so big you could throw a cat through. There was one place to take a shower in the whole village. You carried water from the river, put it in a bucket overhead, and then got under and poured the water on yourself."

Sarah made a face. "So much for hot showers every day."

"Not much of that in the jungle. But God makes it all worthwhile."

After Hank Williams had left, Dixie and Sarah sat and talked about going to Belize.

"Maybe God will send us a lot of four-footed patients," Sarah said, "and we'll make enough money for both of us to make the trip."

"I hope so," Dixie said. "I sure would like to go."

# 4

# THE HOUSE CALL
# IN THE WOODS

**D**ixie stopped in after school to help Aunt Sarah at the animal clinic. She was very busy for a while. A woman had brought in four cats to be dipped and treated.

When the woman left, complaining about the high price of veterinarians, Dixie said angrily, "Why doesn't she bathe her old cats herself?"

Sarah was drying her hands. "That's what veterinarians are for—to do things for animals that people don't want to do themselves." The phone rang just then, and she answered it. "Animal clinic. This is Dr. Logan." She listened awhile, then said, "You'll have to repeat the directions. I'm new in the area." She listened again. "I'll try to get there before dark."

"Who was that?"

"A man named Eagle. He says he has a sick horse." She looked at the notes she had scribbled. "I don't know if I can even find the place."

"I know where that is!" Dixie exclaimed. "I told you about the Eagles. The one where the lady died, and the man and his boy are taking care of the baby."

"Oh, yes, I remember. And you know how to get there?"

"Sure. It's not easy to find, but I know the way."

"I'd better take along everything. It's better to take too much than to leave behind the one thing that you really need."

Twenty minutes later, the Cherokee was loaded with supplies. Aunt Sarah and Dixie pulled out of the clinic parking lot, and Dixie began giving directions. When they reached the last stretch of road, Sarah gasped, "This *is* in the backwoods! I'm glad we've got four-wheel drive."

"It's right past that big grove of trees. There it is. There's the house. See? And that must be the sick horse over there in the corral."

"Fine-looking animal. Well, we'll see what's wrong."

By the time Aunt Sarah stopped the Jeep and they got out, a tall man stepped out of the house.

"Hello, Mr. Eagle," Dixie said. "Remember me?"

Mr. Eagle gaped at her. "You're the girl that fell in the creek."

"That's right. This is my aunt, Sarah Logan."

"Hello, Mr. Eagle." Sarah nodded pleasantly. She put out her hand.

James Eagle shook it briefly. "I've got a sick horse," he said.

"What seems to be the trouble?"

"He stopped eating a couple of days ago . . ."

Sarah and Mr. Eagle walked off toward the horse, which now had his head over the fence, looking at them.

"Hi, Dixie."

Dixie turned around to see Jared. He was holding Dreama. "Oh, let me hold her!"

"You're welcome to do it all you want!" he said with relief in his voice. "I'm not much on baby-sitting."

Dixie took the baby, who was bundled up against the cold air, and began making baby noises at her. She cooed and touched her rosy cheeks. "She's just the sweetest thing."

"Guess so." Jared shrugged. "But she sure is a lot of trouble. Babies are a lot harder to take care of than horses or dogs."

"What a thing to say!"

"They *are* more trouble!" Jared cried. "You don't have to change diapers on a dog. You don't have to fix baby food for a horse."

"I think you're awful!" Dixie told him. "This is the sweetest baby I ever saw. You ought to be thankful to have her."

Jared shifted his feet. "Guess so," he said again. He was wearing a red plaid jacket today, and he buttoned it up closer against the cold wind. "I want to go watch what the doctor does to Capitan."

"You call your horse Captain?"

"No, *El Capitan.* That's Spanish for captain, but I call him Capitan."

Inside the corral, Aunt Sarah was looking down the horse's throat.

Then Mr. Eagle saw Jared. "Get that baby out of the cold, Jared! You ought to have more sense!"

"Aw, Dad, she's all right! She's tough!"

"Mind what I tell you!"

"Come on, Dixie. We'll take her back inside."

Dixie was glad to get out of the cold herself. Inside the Eagle house, she went over to where a fire was burning cheerfully in the large stone fireplace. She backed up to it. "I just love fires."

"You wouldn't love them if you had to cut all the wood and get up and make 'em when it's cold."

"What's the matter with you today, Jared? All you're doing is griping about everything."

Jared looked at her sullenly. "You don't know what it's like. I never get to go anywhere. Neither does Dad. One of us has to stay here all the time and take care of the baby."

Dixie suddenly understood. "What you're really saying is that you miss your mother a lot."

Jared turned the other way.

When he turned back toward her, his face was still sort of squeezed up, and Dixie knew that he had been trying not to cry. She did not know what to say, so she took off Dreama's heavy jumpsuit and soon was playing on the floor with her.

Jared watched them awhile. "You want something to drink?"

"Sure. What have you got?"

"How about Dr. Pepper?"

"My favorite!"

Jared took two cans from the refrigerator. He popped the tops and handed one to Dixie, then sat on the floor with her. He watched her play with Dreama. After a while he said, "Do you want to see my bird?"

"Oh, you have a bird! What is it—a parakeet?"

"No, I wouldn't have one of those things."

"Is it a canary then? They're good for singing."

"No, it's not no canary either."

"Well, what kind of bird is it?"

"I'll show you. But you'll have to put her suit back on."

Dixie, curious about the bird, put the jumpsuit back on the baby. Then she put on her own coat and, carrying Dreama, followed Jared out the back door. He went into a small shed, and when she stepped in behind him, she had to blink since it was darkish inside.

"This is the mew," he said.

"A mew! What's *that*?"

"A place where you keep birds. Here, what do you think of this?"

Dixie's eyes at last were adjusting to the dim light. "What *is* that?"

"It's a peregrine falcon."

"Is it a he or a she?"

"He's a male. That's what falconers call a tiercel."

Dixie moved a little closer.

The bird sat quietly, observing her. He seemed quite relaxed, but she got the impression of strength and hard muscle power. The feathers on his back were slate blue and tightly laid, almost like a coat of armor. He had a pale gray breast that was striped with fine black lines except at his throat. That was a soft salmon pink.

"He's got a funny-looking beak."

"That's what you call a tooth," Jared said. "That's what he kills with."

"He *kills* things?"

"Sure, he kills things! He's a falcon! What did you think they ate? Oatmeal?"

"I don't know much about falcons. He looks so—so strong."

"He *is* strong. And he's the fastest-moving bird there is. Did you know that?"

"No, I didn't."

"Flies faster than anything," Jared told her. "When he's in a dive, he can go up to two hundred miles an hour."

"Wow!" Dixie exclaimed. "That's awfully fast!"

"They can see a long ways, too. Dad says he can see eight times as far as a human."

"Where did you get him?"

"Found him in a nest. A hunter shot the mama and the papa bird."

"That's awful!"

"I hate people that kill falcons. They're good birds." He reached out his hand and stroked the falcon's breast, and the bird raised his wings and made a *"Wichew, wichew!"* sound.

"Come over someday and watch me train him."

"Train him to do what?"

"Don't you know anything about falcons?"

"Well, I did read that they used to have them back in the olden days."

"Kings had them. It was against the law for anybody to have a peregrine in England except the king, or a duke, or somebody

58

like that. They hunted with them. The hunter sees a bird, and the falcon goes after the bird and kills it."

"That seems kind of cruel."

Jared looked at her with disgust. "Lots of animals hunt. Wolves hunt. And tigers. And lions. That's the way they live."

Dixie actually did know all that, but she had never put it together with falcons. She said, "I sure would like to see him fly sometime."

"Well, sure. You can come over and watch."

They got back to the house just as Aunt Sarah and Mr. Eagle were coming in the front door.

"Where have you been with that baby?" his father demanded.

"Just went out to show Perry to Dixie."

"Is that his name? Perry?" Dixie asked. "Why did you name him Perry?"

"Because he's a *pere*grine!"

"I told you, don't be carrying Dreama in and out of the cold!" Mr. Eagle thundered.

Dixie said, "Look, Aunt Sarah, this is Dreama."

Like most women, Aunt Sarah loved

babies. She helped Dixie take off the jump-suit. Then she cuddled the baby and said, "You *are* a sweetheart!" She kissed her on the cheek. "I know you're proud of such a lovely daughter."

Mr. Eagle just grunted and said, "Is the horse going to be all right?"

"I think so. I thought I brought every-thing, but we need some antibiotics that I didn't have. I'll have to bring them back, or you'll have to pick them up."

"It's hard for me to get away!"

The man was so harsh, Dixie thought.

Aunt Sarah said only, "Dixie doesn't live too far from here, and I take her home sometimes. I'll just bring them."

Mr. Eagle merely nodded.

Then Dixie turned to Jared. "I haven't seen you at school."

"I ain't started yet."

"I think schools today are worthless," Mr. Eagle said to Aunt Sarah.

"But Jared has to go to school!" her aunt exclaimed. "That's the law."

"I know it is, and I've been trying to fig-ure out a way to do it. But with only two of us here to take care of Dreama, it's not easy."

"I'm sure it's not. But, really, Jared must go to school. Could you hire a baby-sitter?"

"Who do you know that would want to stay out here in the woods all day?" Mr. Eagle demanded. "Would you want to do it?"

"I *couldn't* do it," Aunt Sarah said.

"No, you couldn't, and you wouldn't, and nobody else would. But I'll try to send the boy in tomorrow."

"That'll be great, Jared," Dixie cried. "We'll be in the same grade. You'll make lots of friends here."

Jared gave his father an odd look. "I never made lots of friends before," he mumbled.

"You will this time," Dixie said. "There are some good kids in our school. You'll like 'em, and they'll like you."

Jared turned to Aunt Sarah, ignoring Dixie. "Is Capitan gonna be all right?"

"I believe he is, Jared!"

"I'm going to get a saddle for him when I get the money. I'm going to train him to do steer roping and bulldogging." His eyes were bright, but then he said, "Of course, saddles cost a lot of money . . ."

"Well, save up for one. You have a beautiful horse there." Aunt Sarah smiled at him. "And you must be very smart to train a horse to do things like that."

"That's about all Indians are good for, isn't it?" Mr. Eagle said bitterly.

Both Dixie and her aunt stared at the man. Dixie wondered again at the harshness in his voice.

Apparently, Aunt Sarah could think of nothing to say. She merely murmured, "Well, I'll bring the medicine by tomorrow."

They left the house without a word of thanks from either Mr. Eagle or Jared.

When they were in the Cherokee, headed toward the Snyder farm, Dixie said, "They have bad manners."

"Yes, they do," Aunt Sarah agreed. "But they have a lot on their minds, raising a baby like that."

"He's real good-looking, isn't he?"

"Who?"

"Mr. Eagle." Dixie suddenly laughed. "I saw you looking at him! I know how you look at guys you think are cute!"

"James Eagle is not cute!"

"No, I guess he's not. But he's tall and . . . and *fine* looking."

"I really didn't notice." Then Aunt Sarah

said with a little smile, "I suppose you think Jared's fine looking, too."

"No, he's cute," Dixie said. She thought for a moment. "But he needs better manners."

# 5

# A LITTLE MISUNDERSTANDING

The morning was cold, but Dixie jumped out of bed, anyway. Shivering, she pulled on her thermal underwear and then a pair of old Lee jeans and a long-sleeved sweatshirt. She brushed her teeth, then hurried downstairs and made herself a quick breakfast.

By the time she had eaten, a horn was blowing in the front yard. She ran outside, grabbing her coat and heavy toboggan cap on the way.

"Hurry up, Dixie! You gonna sleep all day?" Ollie Peck had gotten out of the car marked "Sheriff" and was grinning at her.

"Don't be so impolite to a young lady, son." The friendly sheriff smiled at Dixie. "Get in the back with Blue Boy there. After all your experience with animals, you ought to know all about hounds."

"Hello, Sheriff Peck. Hi, Ollie." Dixie opened the back door and jumped in. A bluetick hound was sitting on the seat. He was a big dog with a light blue-gray coat spotted with darker tints. He licked at her face, and she turned her head away, laughing. "Don't be so affectionate, Blue Boy!"

"He always likes the ladies," Sheriff Peck said. "Can't keep him away from them."

"I'm going to get more birds than Dad this morning, Dixie. You wait and see."

"You're not quite that grown-up yet," the sheriff said.

"Where we going?" Dixie did not really care. She actually did not care anything about quail hunting, but she liked to go out with the sheriff and Ollie.

"I think we'll go over to that open country near Ole River," Sheriff Peck said.

While he drove, Ollie and Dixie talked —mostly about school. Finally, they turned down a dirt road. The car began bumping and throwing Dixie all over the backseat. Blue Boy seemed to like the bumps. When Dixie held onto him, he licked her face again.

Then the sheriff stopped the car. "I was near here last year. Got more birds than I could haul off. Hope we have good luck today."

Dixie got out, and Blue Boy followed her. He at once began sniffing the ground and running around excitedly.

"You just hold your taters, Blue Boy," Sheriff Peck said. He opened the trunk, took out two shotguns, and stuffed his pockets full of shells. After Ollie did the same, the sheriff said, "OK, let's see what we can get."

The air was crisp, and the wind was cold as they crossed the open field. The sun was just rising now, a large crimson disk.

Dixie stayed well behind the two men. She liked to watch Blue Boy run to and fro in wide sweeping circles, sometimes with his nose to the ground, sometimes holding his head high. He just loped along. She said, "I never saw anything move any more *free* than that dog— except maybe a white-tailed deer."

"He's a good dog," Ollie said.

They passed through stands of towering oaks. The leaves were gone now and crackled under their feet.

They came to another large, open field, and Sheriff Peck said, "OK, Ollie. Here's where I filled the bag up last year."

"I'm ready, Dad."

"Remember, now, always keep that gun turned away from whoever's with you. I don't want to have a hunting accident."

"Sure, Dad. I'll do that. Just like you taught me."

This was the part of hunting that Dixie always enjoyed. She liked watching Blue Boy sweep across the field, then stop as if he had been frozen. When that happened, she knew he had found a covey of birds. And she knew he would not move, no matter if a gun went off at his ear, but would stand perfectly rigid as the hunters came up.

Ollie and his dad advanced slowly. Now they were several yards past where Blue Boy remained as fixed as a bronze statue. Suddenly there was a thunderous whirring, and a covey of quail bolted into the air, their wings beating frantically. The guns went off, some birds fell to the ground.

*This is the part of hunting I* don't *like,* Dixie said to herself. *But that's silly, because that's what hunting is.* Still, she always felt sorry for the birds.

Sheriff Peck once told her that most birds did not live to maturity, anyhow. "The coyotes get a lot of them," he said. "Snakes get some. Even wolves. Sometimes coons get the young ones. It's just hard for a young bird to make it. Those that hunters get are just a small percentage."

All morning they traipsed across the hills, and by noon the hunting bags were filled. Even Dixie was carrying one.

"That's enough," Sheriff Peck said. "We'll even have to give some of these away."

As they started back toward the car, Dixie said, "Maybe we could give some to the Eagles. That would be a nice thing to do."

Sheriff Peck just looked at her. Then he said, "Now that you mention it, I've got to make a trip out there anyhow."

Quickly Dixie glanced up at him. It had grown warmer, and he had slung his Mackinaw coat over his shoulder. On the other, he carried a game sack and, under his arm, the shotgun.

"Is there trouble, Sheriff?" she asked.

"His boy has never gone to school. I've gotten a couple of reports, and I've got to go by and talk to Mr. Eagle about it."

"I wish he *would* come to school. You'd like him, Ollie. He's just our age. And he needs a friend."

Ollie grinned up at his father. "Never was any discussion at our house about whether or not *I* would go to school. Dad just took me the first day, plunked me down, and said, 'You sit here until you graduate.'"

"He knew what I meant, all right," Sheriff Peck said. "Youngsters need to be in school. It's the law, anyway."

Dixie got out of the car as soon as it drew up in front of the Eagle house. She waited until the sheriff and Ollie got out, and then the three of them started toward the front door.

It opened before they got there, and Jared's father stepped out to meet them.

"Is this Mr. Eagle?" Sheriff Peck asked.

"That's my name."

"I'm Sheriff Henry Peck." The sheriff stuck out his hand, and Mr. Eagle took it rather slowly. "Sorry to be late getting by to welcome you to the community—I've been pretty busy. But we're glad to have you."

There was a noticeable silence, and for

a moment Dixie did not think Mr. Eagle intended to speak at all.

But then he nodded. "I'm James Eagle. Most folks call me Jim."

"Looks like you've got this place in order, Jim. It always was a nice place. It just needed some work."

At that moment Jared came out and stood beside his father.

"This is my boy, Jared."

"Glad to know you, Jared." Then the sheriff said, "We were out hunting and thought we'd stop by. By the way, you fellows like quail, don't you?"

Suspiciously Jim Eagle nodded. "Sure, everybody likes quail."

"Well, we shot more than I want to clean. Ollie, get some of those birds and give them to Jared. You like to clean birds, Jared?"

"Better than changing diapers."

The sheriff stared. "Well, I guess I would, too. You've got a baby in the house, haven't you?"

"I've got a daughter. My wife died, so Jared and me, we're raising her alone."

"Dixie told me about that. I'm right sorry to hear it."

Ollie came back with a sack of birds and took out a dozen of them. "Here you go, Jared. I'd like to help you clean 'em, but I guess we won't have time."

Jared looked at the birds, then up at his father, who gave him a short nod. "Well, thanks," Jared said. "I don't mind cleaning birds."

The sheriff probably expected to be invited in, but when that didn't happen, he shuffled his feet and then cleared his throat. Then he said, "Been meaning to come by and give that boy of yours a special invitation to go to school."

"You going to arrest him or me?" Mr. Eagle asked grimly.

"Nothing like that," Sheriff Peck said hastily. "But the law is that youngsters have to go to school. I know you've had trouble getting moved in—people always do. But I'd appreciate it if you would see that the boy starts school right away."

A stubborn look crossed Jim Eagle's face. He frowned at Dixie and then looked back at the sheriff. "That vet told you about my boy not being in school?"

"You mean Sarah? No, she didn't tell

me. The folks at the school did. They heard somehow or other."

Dixie could tell that Mr. Eagle was still suspicious of Aunt Sarah, for again he looked sharply at Dixie.

"All right," he said finally. "I'll see that the boy gets to school."

"Well, that's mighty good, Jim. The boy will like it. Need to see more of you, too. Be glad to have you visit church this coming Sunday."

Jim Eagle's face hardened. "I don't go to church."

Dixie could tell that the sheriff heard the hardness in the man's voice. But Sheriff Peck was a wise man. He said only, "Well, if you ever decide to come, you'll sure be welcome. Come on, kids. I've got to get back. More work to do at the office."

At that moment a child's cry came from the house, and Dixie said, "Oh, Sheriff, let me go inside and see Dreama—for just a minute!"

"Go ahead, Dixie. Meantime, maybe Jim will show me around his place."

Dixie went inside. She was followed by Jared, and Ollie came right behind them.

She hurried to the crib and picked up

Dreama. The baby stopped crying at once and started to chortle. "You hate to be left all alone, don't you, Dreama? See, Ollie?" she said, swinging around. "Isn't she sweet?"

"All babies look alike to me," Ollie said.

"Why, that's silly! They don't all look alike any more than big people all look alike. I wish you lived closer, Jared—then I could baby-sit, and you and your dad could go out more."

Jared looked worried about something. "I don't want to go to school," he said. "Nobody will like me."

"Sure they will. Won't they, Ollie?"

Ollie shrugged. "Some will. Some won't. Some of them are real stinkers. I'll be glad to tell you which ones are and which ones aren't."

"Don't you dare, Ollie Peck! That's an awful way to talk about people!"

Ollie grinned. "Might save Jared a lot of time to know who are the good ones and who are the bad ones."

Dixie gave him a disgusted look and turned her attention back to Dreama. And she thought of something. "Jared, why don't you show Perry to Ollie? I'll bet he's never seen a peregrine falcon up close."

"You got one of those?" Ollie asked with interest.

"Come outside, and I'll show you."

Dixie played with Dreama, who was perfectly content in her arms, until the two boys came back.

Ollie was talking excitedly. "I never saw a falcon that close!"

"Some people kill them for sport."

"Not me. And not my dad. It's against the law. Last year he arrested some guys over on the other side of the county for shooting bald eagles. They went to jail and had to pay a fine, too."

"Good," Jared said.

At that moment Sheriff Peck stuck his head in the door. "OK, kids. Time to go."

Reluctantly Dixie gave the baby to Jared. She said, "Jared, if your dad can bring you as far as our house tomorrow, you can ride the bus with us."

Jared's father entered in time to hear this. "I guess that's what we'll do, then." He turned to the sheriff. "Don't have to worry, Sheriff. I'll have the boy in school from now on."

"That's mighty fine," Sheriff Peck said heartily. "You like to hunt?"

"Sure. You ever know an Indian that didn't?"

Sheriff Peck scratched his head and grinned. "Haven't known too many Indians, but I guess they would. How about if you and I team up one of these days and go get some more of these birds? Just the two of us."

Jim Eagle's face softened. Dixie could tell he liked the sheriff. "That sounds good to me. Come by anytime."

Jared watched Dixie and the others drive away. Then he said, "The sheriff's a pretty nice guy, isn't he?"

"Seems to be." He looked down at the boy. "You worried about going to school?"

Jared dropped his head for a moment. He was still holding Dreama, and he touched her dark red hair. Then he looked up and said in a troubled voice, "It's always hard to go to a new place. Some kids are just mean."

Jim Eagle stared at him silently for a moment. Then he said shortly, "Some grown-ups are mean, too." But he added, "Do the best you can. That's all I ask."

# 6

# A TRIP TO THE PRINCIPAL'S OFFICE

Dixie saw Mr. Eagle's black pickup coming, and she waited until it stopped beside her. "Hi, Jared," she said as the boy got out. "How are you, Mr. Eagle?" She glimpsed Dreama in her car seat.

"All right," Jim Eagle said. Then he looked hard at Jared. "Do the best you can, boy."

"Yes sir, I will," Jared said. "Don't worry about me. I'll be home as quick as I can to take care of Dreama."

"Don't worry about her. Just take care of you. Do your work right."

They watched the pickup turn around and head back. "I hate to leave Dreama alone with Dad. It sure ties him down. He can't work much."

"When we have school holidays, I'll

come over and take care of her all day," Dixie said. "I'd like it."

"No holidays coming up soon, but thanks anyway."

"Here comes the bus."

They got on, and Dixie said, "Hi, Mr. Stevens. This is Jared Eagle. He's a new student."

Mr. Stevens was an older man with white hair. "Glad to know you, Jared. Have a seat."

Jared nodded at the driver, then looked nervously down the length of the bus. It was only half filled, but everybody was looking at him.

"There's a couple of good seats near the back," Dixie said. Starting down the aisle, she said loudly, "Hey, everybody, we've got a new student. This is Jared Eagle." She named off a few names, then turned to Jared. "You'll learn them all soon enough."

"Guess so."

They came to an empty seat, and she said, "You sit by the window. I've seen it all a thousand times."

Jared plopped into the seat, scooted over, and Dixie sat beside him. He had his lips pressed tightly together. He said not a word as the school bus rolled down the highway.

From time to time the bus stopped to pick up more students, and eventually it was almost full.

"That's the last one. We go right to school now." Dixie looked over at Jared. "I know you're a little nervous, but don't worry. We'll be in the same classes, I think. You'll have a better time than I did when I came here. I didn't know *anybody*."

"Maybe so, but at least you're not an Indian."

"You don't really think people dislike you because you're an Indian, do you?"

"They act like they do sometimes."

"They act like they don't like *me* sometimes. It's just because some people are mean."

Jared seemed unconvinced.

"We'll go to the office first, Jared," she said when they got to the school.

Dixie led him through the crowd of students making their way toward the school building. When they got to the steps, she saw Billy Joe Satterfield talking with Francine Mosely.

"Hey, what we got here? Fresh meat?"

Billy Joe greeted them. At twelve, Billy was a big boy with red hair. He was also loud and boastful, and Dixie didn't like him much.

"This is Jared Eagle. He just moved in down the road from us. Jared, this is Billy Joe Satterfield. And this is Francine Mosely."

Francine looked coolly at the newcomer. She had auburn hair and brown eyes. Her clothes were obviously very expensive. "What does your father do?" Francine asked Jared.

Jared stared back at the girl, perhaps sensing her arrogance. "He takes care of me and my sister."

"Why doesn't your ma do that?" Billy Joe asked rudely.

"Because she died."

That clearly caught Billy Joe off guard. He said, "Oh. Well, I didn't know that."

"Let's go inside, Jared." Dixie pulled him away, and when they were out of earshot, she said, "They're pretty unbearable, both of them. Francine's folks are nice — and *she* can be, from time to time—but Billy Joe's usually a pain in the neck."

"I could tell that."

In the school office, Dixie introduced Jared to the gray-haired lady behind the counter.

"You'll need one of your parents to come in, Jared," she said.

"I only got my dad. He had to stay home and take care of the baby."

"Well, he will have to come in and sign the papers."

"Can't I take them to him?"

"I'm afraid he will have to come in himself."

"Yes, ma'am. I'll tell him."

"Can't you make him a schedule so he can get started today, Mrs. Simms?"

"I can do that."

"And Mrs. Simms, it would be nice if he could be in most of my classes. That way we could take the same things."

"I'll see what I can do, Dixie."

Dixie waited for Jared, knowing she would be late for her first class. *It won't matter,* she thought. *I always make A's in English, anyhow.*

Mrs. Simms did not take long, and they left the office five minutes later with Jared's schedule.

"Look!" Dixie exclaimed. "You've got all the same classes I have. Mrs. Simms is really nice."

"What about this English teacher?"

"Her name's Mrs. McGeltner. She's kind of a sourpuss. She's a good teacher, but she's pretty strict."

Dixie led the way to Room 106. When they entered, Mrs. McGeltner had already finished taking attendance and was talking about adjectives. She interrupted herself, looked at Dixie, and said sharply, "You're late, Dixie!"

"I'm sorry, Mrs. McGeltner. I was helping Jared here get registered. He's a new student."

"Do you have your schedule, Jared?"

He nodded and handed it to her.

She glanced at it and said, "Fine. You may take that empty desk over there."

The seat was directly in front of Dixie's. To his right sat Billy Joe Satterfield.

Billy Joe grinned at him and said, "Hi, Chief. You didn't bring your bow and arrows?"

"That will be enough, Billy Joe!" Mrs. McGeltner said instantly.

"I was just welcoming the chief to the class, Mrs. McGeltner," he protested. "You always tell us to be polite to people. Well, I'm being polite. This here's Big Chief Eagle. How, Chief. That's the way you Indians talk, isn't it?"

"I talk just like everybody else!" Jared said shortly.

"That will be enough from both of you," Mrs. McGeltner warned in a firm voice. "We're going to study adjectives today . . ."

The lesson went on smoothly until almost the end of the hour. Mrs. McGeltner was going around the room, asking each student to give her a sentence with an adjective in it.

She called on Dixie.

Dixie said, "The tall man walked into the house. *Tall* is an adjective modifying man."

"Very good, Dixie. And now you, Billy Joe."

Billy Joe had been slumped in his seat, apparently bored out of his skull. He straightened up and winked at Francine, who sat to Dixie's left. Then, grinning broadly, he said, "The red Indian kills the dog. *Red* is an adjective modifying Indian. How's that, Chief?"

Jared suddenly flared out, "Why don't you lay off me!"

"What's the matter, Chief? You can't take a little joke?" Unexpectedly, Billy Joe reached across the aisle and grabbed Jared's

85

hair. "You need a feather here so it will stick up—like this!"

"Billy Joe!" That was Mrs. McGeltner.

Jared came to his feet, knocking Billy Joe's arm away. Then he gave him a hard shove.

Overbalanced, Billy Joe's chair tipped over, and he rapped his head hard on the desk behind him.

*"Boys!"*

"Who do you think you're shoving?" Billy Joe yelled. He launched himself at Jared.

The two struggled, knocking off books and pencils amid the screams of the girls and the delighted cries of the boys.

"Stop that at once!" Mrs. McGeltner screamed, but they paid her no attention.

Billy Joe's best friend was Tom Harmon. Tom came out of his chair and leaped on Jared's back.

Dixie jumped up and threw herself at Tom Harmon. She grabbed his hair with both hands and pulled him backwards. Tom let out a scream. He began scuffling with Dixie.

The room was filled with yells and screams. Another desk was knocked over.

Mrs. McGeltner kept on yelling, but her voice was drowned out by all the rest of the noise.

How long this would have gone on no one knew. But suddenly the door opened, and Mr. Thomas, the principal, roared, "*What* is going on here?" He was a big man, usually good-natured, but now he looked angry.

The room got quiet all at once. Then Mrs. McGeltner said, "I'm afraid the new boy started it all!"

"He did not!" Dixie cried. "It was Billy Joe—*he* started it!"

"You're always saying I do things," Billy Joe whined. "It was *his* fault!"

Mr. Thomas looked around the room. "Pick up those desks and chairs, and then everybody sit down!" he ordered. "Mrs. McGeltner, send down to the office those who are responsible."

Dixie well knew what that meant, and ten minutes later she and Jared were sitting outside the principal's office.

"Why aren't the rest of them here?" Jared asked.

"Because they're rich and Mrs. McGeltner pampers them, that's why," Dixie answered. "But Mr. Thomas is fair. He'll listen to us."

"Dad won't like it when he hears about this."

"It's all right. I'll explain how it all was."

The rest of the day, Jared didn't say a word in any of his other classes. Everyone in school seemed to know what had happened.

Billy Joe sneered as he passed by Dixie and Jared in math class. "I guess you redskins know your place now."

"Don't pay any attention to him," Dixie whispered. "He's just trying to start trouble."

Finally the school day was over.

Just before the bus came to Dixie's stop, she looked out and saw Mr. Eagle's pickup. "There's your dad. Let me explain to him."

When they got off the bus, they went to where Mr. Eagle was leaning against the fender of the pickup.

"How was it?" he asked.

"It wasn't so good, Mr. Eagle," Dixie said. "There was a big fuss in English class. But it wasn't Jared's fault." She went on to explain.

Then Jared said, "It really *wasn't* my fault, Dad. But you should have seen Dixie and Ollie. They jumped right in on my side. If the principal hadn't come, we'd have whooped them all."

Mr. Eagle scowled. "I didn't have much fun when I went to school myself. I guess you can't just take it every day, can you, Jared?"

"You're not mad at me, Dad?"

"No, not if what Dixie says is the straight of it. Come on home. Dreama's missed you."

Jared went around the truck and got in beside the baby carrier.

Mr. Eagle looked down at Dixie. "Thanks a lot, Dixie. I appreciate what you did for Jared."

"I know you're worried, but it'll be all right."

Mr. Eagle shook his head. "I doubt it." He got into the truck and drove off without looking back.

Dixie watched them go. She felt bad about the whole thing. "I'll tell Aunt Sarah what happened. We've got to do something to help the Eagles!"

# 7

# THE FALCON

Jared's father was frowning again. "You mean to tell me," he asked slowly, "that you got into a fight on your first day of school?"

"Wasn't my fault, Dad. Like I told you, I didn't start it."

"So who did start it?"

His dad listened without saying a word as Jared told the story yet again. When Jared finished, he said, "And Dixie and this boy Ollie got in on your side?"

"That's right, Dad." Jared nodded eagerly. "Billy Joe Satterfield, he has a lot of friends, and some of them started to jump on me. If it hadn't been for Dixie, and Ollie, and *their* friends, they would have beaten me to a pulp."

Mr. Eagle was holding Dreama in his

lap. He smiled down at her. Then he looked back at Jared. "It looks to me like you've got both friends and enemies."

"I guess so, Dad."

"Everything's not always fair in this world. It helps to have some friends."

Anxious to change the subject, Jared said, "Well, when I'm in school, I don't see how you're going to take care of Dreama all the time."

"May have to hire somebody. I'm going to have to go to work full-time sooner or later."

The phone rang at that instant, and Jared picked it up.

"Hello, Jared. This is Dixie."

"Oh, hi, Dixie. I was just telling Dad more about the mess we had at school."

"I told Aunt Sarah about it, too. She thinks it's awful. And she wants to do something nice for you and your dad."

"Like what?"

"Let her talk to him. Is he there?"

"Sure." Jared handed the telephone to his father. "It's Dixie. Her aunt wants to talk to you."

An odd light came into his dad's eyes, but he took the phone and said gruffly,

"Hello!" He listened for a few moments, then said, "I guess that'll be all right. It's sure something you don't have to do . . . All right. I'll see you then." He handed the phone back to Jared and then stood up, still holding Dreama.

"What was it, Dad?"

"That woman vet—she's coming out and bringing Dixie with her. They're going to cook supper for us!"

"Yay, that's great!" Jared shouted. "Nothing against you, Dad, but I get tired of the same old stuff all the time."

His father managed a smile. "I get tired of yours, too. And I guess we'd better clean this place up. We don't want her to think we live in a rats' nest."

"This seasoning was a secret recipe of my grandmother's." Aunt Sarah was standing at the cookstove, sprinkling spices over the steaks that sizzled in the frying pan. "I'm the only one that has it now.'"

"If it's any good," Jim Eagle said, "you'd better give it to me. Then if you die, it won't go with you to your grave."

"Don't talk like that, Dad!" Jared said. "Not about dying and stuff."

Quickly Jim Eagle looked at his son. He said, "I was just kidding, Jared."

"Well, I'll be glad to share the recipe with you if you want it." Sarah poked at the steaks with a fork and said, "This is certainly tender venison."

"Nice fat deer. I just shot him yesterday," Jim Eagle noted.

"But it's not deer season," Sarah protested after a moment. She looked over at Jim Eagle, who merely grinned back at her. "You can get fined for hunting out of season —as you well know. I wouldn't tell it around if I were you."

"You're not going to turn me in, are you, Sarah?"

"Of course not!" Aunt Sarah snapped indignantly. "Here—all of you get your plates, and we'll eat cafeteria style. Just pick out the steaks you want."

Soon the four of them were sitting at the table. Dixie had baked potatoes, and they had opened cans of corn and green beans. Aunt Sarah had made large pieces of Texas toast, and a delicious aroma filled the air.

"I'll hold you on my lap," Dixie said to Dreama, who was crawling and pulling herself up at Dixie's knee.

As soon as Dixie had the baby in her lap, Aunt Sarah said, "Do you want to say the blessing, Jim?"

Mr. Eagle stared at her as if she had asked a strange thing. "I guess so," he mumbled. He bowed his head and awkwardly said a few words. Then, as if with relief, he said, "Well, it's good to eat somebody's cooking other than our own, isn't it, Jared?"

"Sure is, Dad." Jared sliced open his potato and pulverized it with his fork. He put a huge glob of butter on top. Then he took the salt shaker in one hand and the pepper in the other and began seasoning it.

"You shouldn't eat that much salt, Jared!" Aunt Sarah cried. "It's not good for you."

"It tastes good, though." He grinned.

"No sense trying to reform him," his father said. "He's too much like me."

Dixie's aunt looked around the room and said, "You do good housekeeping for a pair of bachelors. I will say that for you."

"You should have seen it before we cleaned it up," Jared volunteered. He talked around a forkful of potato. "It was the biggest mess you ever saw. Dad made me help clean it up because you were coming."

Jim Eagle looked embarrassed. "Man just wasn't made to clean house," he said. He started to say something else, but he changed his mind and cut off a bite of steak instead.

Dixie was sure that he had almost said something about his dead wife. There was hurt in his eyes, and she knew that he was still very lonely.

"One thing I can't understand," Mr. Eagle said, "is how anybody can cook and take care of a baby at the same time. I usually either burn everything to a crisp or else forget to put it on while I'm taking care of Dreama."

"Maybe women just naturally do that better than men," Sarah said. She tasted her venison and cocked her head to one side. "Not bad. How do you like the seasoning?"

"Give me the recipe," Mr. Eagle said. He smiled at her, and his face relaxed.

To Dixie, Jared's father had always seemed a rather tense man. It was as if he was on guard at all times and not ready to let anybody into his private life. But as the meal continued, he acted more and more relaxed. And by the time Aunt Sarah got up to serve the coconut pie that they had brought with them, everyone seemed very comfortable indeed.

"I'm going to pop if I eat this piece of pie!" Jared declared. "Stand back, everybody!"

They all laughed, and then Dixie said, "Jared, sometime I want you to show Aunt Sarah how beautiful Perry is when he flies."

"Don't get him started on that bird!" his father said. "He's out there in that mew with him all the time."

"It's kind of a miracle to me," Sarah said, "that a wild bird can be taught to come back. It looks like they'd just fly off the first chance they got."

"It takes lots of patience." Mr. Eagle took another bite of pie and then a sip of coffee. "Not something you can do in a hurry."

After everyone was finished with dinner, Dixie said, "Why don't you two go shopping or something? Jared and I can baby-sit."

A startled look came into Jim Eagle's eye. Some of the tenseness returned. "I don't think your aunt would like to be seen in the company of a redskin."

Sarah flushed and said angrily, "That's the dumbest thing I ever heard you say, Jim Eagle, and it's insulting too!"

"Insulting? What do you mean?"

"I mean that you're suggesting that I'm prejudiced, and I'm not!"

"You mean you'd be seen in the mall with an Indian?"

"Yes, I would," she said firmly. "I have no problem with that at all."

"Well, anyway, why don't you two go on?" Dixie said. "Jared says you don't get to go places much, Mr. Eagle. We can feed Dreama and play with her and watch TV— or maybe play Monopoly, if you've got the game."

"We've got the game, and I never lose," Jared announced.

"Well, I never lose either," Dixie said. "So one of us is going to get a lesson."

Stopping the pickup in front of the house, Jim Eagle said, "That was quite a shopping excursion. I never spent so much time not buying anything." He shut off the engine.

They sat in the cab for a while. Outside the moon was full, and the woods were silent. Light flooded out of the windows onto the ground, and Sarah could hear music playing.

"All that advertising in front of the theater—it made me feel funny," she said thoughtfully. "Some of the richest people in the world got on that boat. And they didn't know they would never get to the other side. They were told that was the one ship that couldn't be sunk, but it did sink."

"It shows you can't count on anything."

"You can count on some things," she said.

Sarah had enjoyed her evening with Jared's father. They had walked in the mall for a couple of hours, then stopped off at Baskin Robbins for ice cream, as late as it was. She suddenly realized that she had not had such a good time in years.

Suddenly he turned to her and asked, "Why haven't you ever married, Sarah?"

Taken off guard, Sarah turned her face away and looked out into the moonlit woods. "I don't know. I just never found anybody I wanted to spend my whole life with, I suppose."

"I did once."

Sarah looked quickly back at the tall man who sat beside her. "You must have loved your wife very much."

"Yes, I did. We were very happy." He said nothing for a long time, then heaved a sigh. "Losing her has been hard on me, but sometimes I think it's been even harder on Jared."

"It would be hard on both of you, I'm sure. She was a Christian, Jared told me."

"Yes, she was." He paused. "I guess I got mad at God when she died. That's kind of dumb, isn't it?"

"It's not the wisest thing in the world. God knows more than we do about things like that. I think you need to be a little bit more open to letting God heal the pain."

And suddenly Jim Eagle began to talk about his wife. He told Sarah how they had met, how they had married, the happiness they'd had. And when the children came, what a joy that had been. When he stopped, he looked at her with surprise on his face. "I've never talked to anybody like this. Not since Kathy died."

"God can heal the wounds, Jim," she said.

Jim Eagle said nothing for a moment. Then, "Maybe He can," he said, "but I've been pretty upset with Him."

Sarah said, "We'd better get inside. It's getting late, and I have to go to work tomorrow."

Soon she and Dixie were on their way home.

"Did you have a good time?" Dixie asked.

"Yes, I did. To my surprise. He's a very fine man. He's deeply upset over the loss of his wife."

"So is Jared. He's very lonesome for a mother."

They drove on in silence for a while, and Sarah kept thinking about the three that remained back in the old house.

# 8

# MR. EAGLE'S SURPRISE

Look who just came in the door!" Manny said softly.

Dixie was sitting in her usual place, close to the front, waiting for church to start. She had been reading a song in the hymnbook.

She twisted around casually and blinked with surprise. "Why, it's the Eagles!"

"Sure is," Manny said. He was wedged between Dixie and his father. "I guess all your preaching at them did some good."

Dixie was happy to see the Eagles in church. She saw, however, that they looked uncomfortable, and she began sliding out of the pew.

"*Ow!*" Uncle Roy said. "That's my foot you stepped on! Where are you going?"

"I'm going to help the Eagles get settled."

She hurried up the aisle and greeted Mr. Eagle and Jared and baby Dreama with a big smile. "Hello! I'm glad to see you here." Dixie had no sooner said this than the pastor came up behind her. "Pastor Stone, this is Mr. Eagle, and this is Jared, and this is Dreama."

Smiling broadly, Pastor Stone reached out a hand. "Glad to see you. Dixie's been telling me about you, Mr. Eagle. I was on my way out to pay you a visit tomorrow morning."

Jim Eagle shifted Dreama to his other arm and shook the pastor's hand. "We don't get out much."

"There's a nursery," Dixie said. "Let Jared and me take Dreama down." She reached out her arms, and the baby came willingly. "You bring the diaper bag, Jared. Pastor Stone will find Mr. Eagle a good seat somewhere up front."

"Not up front!" Jim Eagle said. He looked *very* uncomfortable. "Just along the side—or even in the back."

On the way to the nursery, she said, "I'm really glad you came, Jared. Whose idea was it?"

"Dad's," Jared admitted. "He got up

this morning and looked at me and said, 'Jared, we're going to church. Get yourself ready.' Just like that."

They arrived at the nursery at that moment, and Mrs. Henry cooed over Dreama. When Jared said that she might cry, Mrs. Henry laughed. "I've been taking care of crying babies all my life! Now you two run along to church."

Dixie grabbed him by the arm. "Let's hurry. We don't want to miss the singing."

When they stepped inside the auditorium, Dixie swept it with a glance. "There's your dad over there. I'll sit with you." She led the way to a pew halfway back. Jared sat next to his dad.

The song service began almost at once, and when they sang "Amazing Grace," Dixie looked around Jared at Mr. Eagle. "You have a pretty voice, Mr. Eagle! You must have sung a lot," she whispered.

"Not much lately," he whispered back.

"He used to be in a quartet," Jared said. "That was before Mom died."

Dixie thought that was sad. "If I had a voice as good as yours, I'd sing all day long. I do anyway." She laughed. "Even if I can't sing a lick."

"Will you please hush up there? Church has started!"

Dixie looked around and saw Mrs. McGeltner seated right behind them. A frown was on her face.

"I'm sorry, Mrs. McGeltner," Dixie whispered. "I wasn't thinking."

The song service went on, and several people turned around to see who had such a beautiful voice.

After the singing, Pastor Stone preached about the Prodigal Son. As always, it was a fine message.

The minute church was over, Dixie said, "You're to come home and have dinner with us. You haven't tasted *my* cooking yet."

"Oh, we couldn't do that, Dixie!" Mr. Eagle said hastily. "Thank you, anyway."

But Dixie practically hauled Mr. Eagle and Jared to where her uncle and aunt were coming up the aisle. She announced, "I invited the Eagles to have dinner with us, like you said."

Uncle Roy beamed. He shook hands with Jim Eagle and then winked at Dixie. "The cooking's not too good at our house, but I make out the best I can."

"Roy Snyder," Aunt Edith said, "you know you get the best cooking in the county with Dixie in the kitchen."

"I know it. I was just teasing. Come on. These long-winded preachers make me hungry."

Dixie quickly and efficiently prepared crispy, golden brown fried chicken, mashed potatoes and gravy, fresh biscuits, and a green bean casserole. For dessert she served her favorite chocolate cake.

As they finished the cake and ice cream, Mr. Eagle leaned back and said wistfully, "That was a fine meal. Both of you ladies are great cooks."

"Why, thank you, Mr. Eagle." Aunt Edith smiled sweetly. "Dixie *is* a fine cook."

"Second best in the world," Uncle Roy said. This time he winked at Mr. Eagle. "I guess you know who the first is."

Jared said, "Could I have another piece of cake?"

"Jared, you're going to pop!" his father protested.

Jared grinned broadly. "Well, give me the cake and then stand back."

Uncle Roy got up. "How about a walk, and I'll show you around the place, Jim?"

"Fine. I'd like to see it."

The men were gone for a long time. Dixie and Aunt Edith washed the dishes. Jared lay on the floor, watching TV and playing with Dreama.

Finally laying her apron aside, Dixie went into living room and said, "Let's go outside, Jared."

"I'll watch the baby," Aunt Edith said. "I just love little girls."

"Remember that the next time you want to paddle me!" Dixie laughed and ran out the door, grabbing her coat on the way.

"I wonder where Dad and your uncle went?" Jared said, looking around.

They searched for some time and finally found the two men standing over in a valley that was half filled with water. Dixie's uncle was saying, "This land's practically useless, Jim. It floods every time a heavy dew comes." Uncle Roy sighed. "Too bad, too. It would raise some fine crops if it just wasn't so wet."

"That shouldn't be hard to fix," Mr. Eagle said. He looked over the terrain. "All you have to do is dam up that ravine over there. That's where all your water's coming from. If you put a dam right there, it would run the water toward the creek, and then you could farm this land."

"Well, I'll be dipped," Uncle Roy said, "if you ain't right!" He took off his red hunting cap and scratched his head. "But I don't know how to do a thing like that."

"I do."

"*You* know how?"

"Sure, Dad's an engineer," Jared spoke up. "He can do anything like that. Build dams, or roads, or bridges . . ."

Dixie and her uncle stared at the tall man with the bronze face.

"Is that right?" Uncle Roy asked. "Are you really one of them engineer fellows?"

"I was once. Haven't done much lately." He seemed embarrassed by their admiration. "But if you really want to do this, I'll rent a small bulldozer and come over and dam it up for you."

"How much would it cost?"

"Nothing for me. Just the rent of the dozer. Shouldn't be too much. I think I can do it in three or four days. But somebody would have to baby-sit Dreama."

"Well, shoot, I'll do that myself! Or

keep Dixie out of school and let her do it," Uncle Roy said.

"Oh, good! I'd much rather play with Dreama than go to school!"

Uncle Roy scratched his head. "On second thought, your aunt would never let us do that. I reckon she and I together could keep one baby, though, if you'd be good enough to help me, Jim."

"No problem."

"Tomorrow's a holiday," Dixie said. "I can keep Dreama that day."

"I'll come over, too," Jared said. "I'll bring Perry, and I'll show you how to fly him."

The next day was one of the best days Dixie Morris had ever had. It was exciting to watch Mr. Eagle push the dirt around with the bulldozer. Once he even let her climb up on the seat with him.

"There's no steering wheel!" she said.

"Nope. You just put on the brake on the right side, and it turns right. Put on the brake on the left, and it turns left. Have a try."

Dixie wasn't very good at it, but she could turn the bulldozer. And it was fun to watch the dirt pile up in front of the blade.

She watched as Jared took his turn.

Then the two of them went out to where Jared had put Perry. It was an old henhouse that Uncle Roy didn't use anymore.

"I'm going to show you something about falcons," he said. "First, you've got to put on this gauntlet." He handed it to her. "It goes on your arm. I tried handling Perry once without it, and his talons went in to the bone—anyway, it felt like it."

Dixie fastened the leather gauntlet to her left forearm the way Jared showed her.

Then he took her to where the beautiful falcon was sitting quietly on a perch. "Hold your arm up, and he'll step out on it."

Dixie had never really been this close to a falcon before, but she held her arm close to the bird. And as Jared had said, Perry immediately stepped onto it. Even through the gauntlet, she could feel his powerful talons close about her wrist.

"If I didn't have this on, I'd hate to know what he'd do to my arm."

"He wouldn't mean to hurt you," Jared said, "but those talons are needle sharp. Now, let me put this hood on him."

Dixie watched him slip a little cover over the falcon's eyes. "What's that for?"

"He's trained to go after his prey when the hood's removed," Jared said. "Let's go down to that big field. We're bound to see something there for him to catch."

When they reached the field, he nodded. "See. There's a couple of big old crows. All they're good for is to eat the farmers' corn, anyhow. Now we'll get him ready."

He pulled off the hood. In the bright sunlight, Perry raised himself slightly and spread his wings, but he did not fly. He turned his head and looked at Dixie.

"I'll scare up one of those crows," Jared said. "Let it get into the air about fifty feet. Then raise your arm in a throwing motion, and Perry will take off."

Dixie's heart was racing. She saw an enormous crow fly upward, calling, *"Caw, caw!"* She waited until he was higher. She swung her arm upward. The falcon's pinions began to beat the air. Then the peregrine soared skyward, faster than she had thought possible, until he was just a dot against the blue.

Jared ran back. "Watch him now," he said. "He's going to stoop."

"What?"

"He's going to dive. See? There he goes!"

The falcon had his wings folded back. He was falling like a meteor.

In her excitement, Dixie grabbed Jared's arm. She watched as Perry struck the crow, and Jared said, "That's all for Mr. Crow."

"You mean he's dead?"

"Probably. When a peregrine hits, he usually kills his prey with the first blow. They're traveling, sometimes, two or three hundred miles an hour, and that just kills whatever he hits."

Dixie always hated to see anything killed. Still, killing a *crow* did not seem so bad a thing.

They ran to where the bird was sitting and beginning to eat.

"We usually keep him a little hungry. That way they hunt better," he said. He grinned at Dixie. "It's a little messy. Are you sure you want to watch?"

Actually Dixie didn't. But she made herself watch and was surprised that a falcon's feeding was not as messy as she had thought.

Soon they were on their way home. The peregrine was once again riding on Dixie's arm. She stroked him, and he lifted his wings and made a mewling sound deep in his chest.

"He's a beautiful bird," she whispered. "I don't see how you ever trained him to come back to you. I'd think any wild thing would just go away and never come back."

"It takes a long time. And you have to keep them on a line at first or they *will* try to fly away. But give them a little meat when they do come, and make a noise, and they'll come to you all right."

They were almost to the Snyder house when Jared said suddenly, "It looks like I'm not going to get that new saddle for Capitan. Dad says money's pretty scarce."

"I still don't have enough money to go on that trip to Belize, either."

"I've been reading about Belize. They say the second biggest barrier reef in the world is off the Belize coast. Wouldn't it be great to go snorkeling down there? Think of the fish you'd see."

"I've never snorkeled except in a swimming pool."

The two kept on walking. Then Jared

abruptly said, "I just don't see how we're going to do it, Dixie. The money, I mean."

"We'll just keep on praying. If God wants me to go to Belize, and if He wants you to have a saddle, then He sure knows how to take care of that."

# 9
# A BAD DAY
# IN THE WOODS

The sun was starting downward as Dixie and Jared trudged across the barren field. Over to their right loomed the cliffs of Bear Mountain, and underneath their feet the dead stubble crackled noisily.

"I sure am tired," said Dixie.

Jared grinned. "Girls just aren't as tough as boys," he bragged. He took her arm. "I'll give you a tow."

"Take your grubby hands off me!" Dixie jerked her arm away. It irritated her that Jared could walk farther than she could, and she purposed to work hard to get in better shape.

Jared didn't appear to be offended. "We didn't get many squirrels," he said, "but we got enough for one meal for all of us." He hefted the canvas bag that hung on a strap about his neck. "And I don't see why you don't want to kill anything, but you'll eat whatever *I* kill."

"I wish you would hush!" Dixie said. She knew it was unreasonable not to eat game that was taken by hunters. But still it gave her a queasy feeling if she thought about what she was eating.

They came to Tinker Creek. It was almost dry, and they leaped across easily. Just as they did, a gun sounded.

"That was close! I wonder who's shooting. And at what."

"Maybe someone else hunting squirrels."

They kept walking toward the base of Bear Mountain. When they emerged from a thicket, Dixie stopped. "It's Billy Joe Satterfield."

"Sure is," Jared said. "And he's shot something. Let's go see what he got."

The boy was looking at something on the ground, and Dixie and Jared were within twenty feet of him before he heard them and whirled. "I—I thought it was a quail," he said.

Jared went close enough to see what Billy Joe had shot. "That's a falcon!" he said angrily. He glared at Billy Joe. "You killed a *falcon!*"

Billy Joe's face was pale. His mouth opened and shut like a fish's. "I—I didn't mean to. I didn't think I could hit it. I just wanted to scare him. I didn't even know what it was!"

Dixie came up as Jared went to the bird. It was a still mass of feathers. He looked up. "You killed a falcon! That's against the law. You're going to go to jail."

Billy Joe Satterfield swallowed hard. To Dixie's astonishment, he began to tremble. "Don't tell on me," he begged. "Please don't tell. You know how bad Sheriff Peck hates people that kill anything out of season."

"Peregrine falcons are always out of season!" Jared said grimly. He stood up. "And what's worse, this is a female. She's probably got chicks somewhere up in that mountain."

Dixie looked sorrowfully at the dead bird. "She's so beautiful, and now she's dead," she whispered. Then she too snapped at Billy Joe, "I hope you do go to jail, Billy Joe Satterfield!"

Billy Joe seemed paralyzed with fright.

"It was an accident," he kept saying over and over. He didn't mean to kill the bird.

"How can it be an accident if you pointed the gun at the falcon and pulled the trigger? You did it on purpose!" Jared told Billy Joe Satterfield exactly what he thought of him.

Billy Joe gulped and turned to Dixie. "Dixie, don't let him tell anybody. You're my friend. I didn't *know* it was a falcon."

Dixie had never liked Billy Joe Satterfield. But she could not help feeling sorry for him. It was clear to her that he hadn't been trying to shoot a protected bird. She said, "Jared, I don't see it would do any good to tell on him!"

"Do any good? They'd put him where he wouldn't shoot any more falcons! The boys' reform school—that's what would do some good!"

Looking at Billy Joe's agonized expression, Dixie said, "Well, he won't do it again."

"How do you know he won't do it again?"

"I won't! I promise I won't! Never again! I won't shoot *any* birds!" For a while they stood there under the trees, Jared grim faced and determined, Billy Joe in tears, and Dixie trying to convince Jared that telling on Billy Joe would do nobody any good.

"Didn't *you* ever make a mistake, Jared?" Dixie asked at last.

"Sure, I made mistakes, but not like this one!"

But finally Dixie prevailed, and when Jared reluctantly agreed to keep quiet about it, she said to Billy Joe, "You bury the bird."

"I don't have a shovel!"

"Then dig with your fingernails," she said. "Let's go, Jared."

"Where we going?" Jared asked.

"We're going to find her nest."

Jared looked toward the steep cliff. "They're pretty hard to find and hard to get to. Dad and I climbed up a cliff when we found Perry. But I'm telling you, it was scary getting up and down again."

Nevertheless, Dixie prevailed again, and they left Billy Joe digging a hole with his pocketknife. "Bury her deep," Dixie said. "I'll come back and check." Then she and Jared walked off.

They searched hard for the nest. It was already late afternoon. But finally Jared spotted it, high on a sharp peak. They scrambled up the steep incline and came to the nest.

Dixie, out of breath, dirt all over her face, and fingers sore from clambering up the stony slope, murmured, "There's just one."

"The others may have already flown out. This one's about ready to fly."

"We'll have to take her with us."

"You take the game bag," Jared said, "and I'll carry the chick."

"Will do." Dixie watched him warily reach in and snare the bird, which began to squawk. "Is it a male or a female?"

"A female, I think. Hard to tell when they're this young. Dad will know."

They climbed down carefully and retraced their steps. When they came to where the mother falcon had been killed, they found the grave.

"I'd like to punch that Billy Joe Satterfield out," Jared muttered.

"I know it's hard not to feel bad toward him, but we can't."

"*I* can!"

"Let's go tell your dad what happened."

They reached the Eagle house, totally exhausted.

Mr. Eagle took one look at the bird and said, "Why did you take her out of the nest?"

Dixie looked at Jared, and finally he said, "The mother got killed."

"Got killed how?"

"A hunter," Jared said.

Mr. Eagle looked closely at them. "I know neither one of you would kill a falcon. But you're shielding *somebody*. And that may not be a good thing. The law's made for things like this."

Dixie said tentatively, "I know, Mr. Eagle. But it was really an accident, and he'll never do it again. I guarantee it."

"All right, then." Jim Eagle took the fledgling in his hands, and then he grinned. "She's a pretty good specimen."

"Is it a female?"

"Sure is. You two will have to think of a name for her."

Several weeks went by after the capture of the baby falcon. Dixie went every day to see the bird's progress. She learned how to begin its training, and Jared assured her the peregrine was just the right age.

Dixie watched him put a lightweight nylon string on the falcon. He would throw out meat and let her fly to it. Then he would urge her back to him afterward. For a while there seemed to be no progress.

But Jared assured her, "One of these days we can turn her loose, and she'll go and then come back."

One afternoon as Dixie watched Jared patiently train the fledgling, she said, "I bet most people don't know *anything* about how falcons are trained."

"Most don't."

And that's when Dixie had an idea. "Jared!" she exclaimed. "I know how we can get money for your saddle and enough for me to go on the mission trip to Belize."

Jared looked skeptical. He was holding the falcon and gently stroking her feathers. "How are you going to do that?"

"You know that magazine *Young American?*"

"Sure. I read it all the time. It's got lots of good stuff in it about animals."

"That's what I was thinking. Did you read about the contest?"

"No, I haven't seen the last issue. What kind of contest?"

"They're offering a thousand dollars first prize for the best story about an animal with pictures to go along with it."

Jared's jaw dropped. "And I know what you're thinking! I can read your mind!"

"Jared!" Dixie said excitedly. "We could get pictures of you training this falcon and then some of Perry too."

"I don't even have a camera!"

"My aunt has one. It's got a telephoto lens. It can take any kind of pictures. I've used it lots of times."

"You think she'd let us use it?"

"Sure she will. She might even help us write the story." But then Dixie shook her head. "No, that's against the rules. *We* would have to do the writing."

Jared scratched his jaw. "I'm not very good at writing."

"But I am. You tell me what's happening, and I'll write it down. Oh, Jared," she exclaimed, "I just know we're going to win!"

"I wish we could," he said slowly.

They stared at each other, and suddenly both laughed out loud.

"We must be crazy," Jared said, "but I sure would like to have that saddle for Capitan."

"And I want to go to Belize."

# 10

# THE FALL OF
# THE SPARROW

As winter's last gloomy days passed and spring began to come, Dixie and Jared spent many hours with the fledgling falcon. It seemed to Dixie that the magnificent bird grew bigger every day. And more and more she was fascinated with how Jared and his father were able to train the birds.

They had named the falcon Sunlight, for sometimes her feathers gleamed as bright as the sun. She seemed to get along well with Perry, although they were always kept on separate perches.

Dixie had practically assumed owner-ship of Aunt Sarah's camera. She was using all of her pocket money for film and had taken roll after roll, capturing the fledgling in every stage of development. She and Jared also took pictures of Perry as he soared in the sky and hurtled down on his prey.

One day the two of them were sitting on the living-room floor at Jared's house. They had spread out the best pictures and were trying to decide which ones to have enlarged and send in with their story. "I don't have money to buy any more film," Dixie complained.

"I've got enough for another roll," Jared said, "but how many more do we have to *have?*"

"I don't know. It seems you have to take a hundred pictures to get two or three good enough to win a contest with."

He picked up a photograph and studied it. "It looks to me like *this* one ought to win the contest."

Dixie moved in closer to see.

"That *is* good," she said. "I remember the day we took it."

The picture was of Perry diving. His talons were extended and his wings spread full width. Beneath him was a rabbit. *You can see every hair on the rabbit,* Dixie thought. She could almost feel its nose twitching.

"We've got to use this one," Dixie said. "You still miss your mother?"

Jared was so surprised at the totally unexpected question that he put down the picture. "Why are you asking *that*?"

"I mean, I miss my dad and my mom, and I guess you miss your mother, too. Don't you?"

"*Of course, I miss my mother!* What do you think I am?"

But something had been on Dixie's mind a long time. "Maybe you could have another mother."

"What do you mean, 'another mother'? There aren't any more mothers."

"Well, I mean your dad—he might want to get married again."

"I don't want any other mother!"

Dixie looked steadily at Jared. "I was thinking maybe he might marry Aunt Sarah."

Jared looked at her as if she had fallen out of a tree. "He's not going to marry *anybody!*"

"Don't you have any romance in your soul?"

"No, I don't!" Jared said. "And you got a great deal too much of it, if you want to know. My dad's not going to marry your aunt. Period."

"Well, it *might* happen. And it wouldn't be bad, you know. Then we'd be in the same family—sort of cousins. That would be neat, wouldn't it?"

"You don't know what my dad should do!"

"I know he misses your mom. And I know you need a woman around the house. This place would be a mess all the time if Aunt Sarah and I didn't clean it up!"

Just then Dixie's aunt came in, carrying Dreama. She was closely followed by Jared's father.

Jared looked at them suspiciously.

Aunt Sarah's face was serious. "I've got some bad news, I'm afraid." She put Dreama down, and the baby immediately crawled to Dixie.

Dixie took her in her arms. "What bad news, Aunt Sarah?"

"Capitan's not doing very well."

Jared's eyes widened. "What's wrong with him now?"

"I'm not quite sure, Jared. I've never seen anything exactly like it." She stooped down beside him.

"But you can make him well, can't you, Miss Sarah?"

"I wish I could say yes for sure, but I'm going to do my best." She squeezed Jared's shoulders. "And we'll trust the Lord."

Aunt Sarah went to the kitchen then to begin supper. She was cooking for the Eagles tonight.

Before Dixie went to help, Jared said quickly, "Dixie, I'm wondering something . . ."

"What?"

He got up from the floor and stood staring down at the pictures that Dreama was considering getting into. "I'm wondering," he said slowly, "if God really cares anything about horses."

She nodded emphatically. "He cares about *anything* that has to do with us. It's just like your father. If something bad is happening to you, he'd want to fix it. Well, that's the way God is."

Jared did not answer for so long that Dixie wondered if he had forgotten the conversation. But at last he said, "Do you really think so?"

"I don't *think* so. I *know* so. It's what the Bible says." She took his arm. "I'll tell you what. I've been praying about winning this contest. Why don't I just pray that God will make Capitan well?"

"Go ahead. God wouldn't listen to me."

Dixie looked into the boy's face and said quietly, "You think He doesn't care about you? He even knows when one sparrow falls. And you're worth more than any old sparrow."

Jared again was silent. Then he said, "If God would make Capitan well, I think I could believe in Him with all my heart."

"You remember that," Dixie said, "because right now I'm starting to pray for Capitan to be healed. But just remember, Jared—God is here, and He cares about you whether your horse gets well or not."

## 11
# SOMETHING NEW FOR JARED

When spring came, Dixie Morris found herself busier than she had ever been in her entire life. It seemed there were never enough hours in the day to get everything done.

She rose early every morning and fixed breakfast for her uncle and aunt. Then she grabbed her books and ran to catch the bus. She and Jared always chatted all the way to school about Perry and the fledgling.

At school, it seemed all the teachers had gotten together and decided to assign as much homework as possible. Dixie groaned along with the other students every time Mrs. McGeltner said, "I want you to write a theme."

She complained to Jared on the way home. "I know it isn't so, but it does *seem* she doesn't want to do anything but make life miserable for us."

"You got that right," Jared grumbled. "She couldn't possibly *read* all these things."

"Sometimes I think she assigns stuff just to be mean—but then I think, *No, she really wants to help us become better writers.*"

This time Jared did not answer. They had just gotten off the bus, and she realized that he had said hardly a word all the way. "What's the matter, Jared?"

"Capitan is worse. I can tell by the way he looks."

"Should Aunt Sarah look at him again?"

"She was there day before yesterday. I don't think she's helping much."

"She's doing all she can!" Dixie said defensively.

"Oh, I know that!" He shifted his book pack from one shoulder to the other. "It's just that I get afraid he won't ever get well."

"I want to go home with you and see him. Wait till I go in and ask Aunt Edith."

"I'll wait."

Capitan was standing in the pasture with his head down.

136

"He's not eating right," Jared said, "and he's lost weight."

Dixie always felt bad when any animal was sick. She went to the fence and called Capitan, but he did not even look at her. *He does look bad,* she thought, but she didn't want to make Jared feel any worse. "Aunt Sarah says sometimes horses get like this and then they get better all at once."

Jared gazed at his horse gloomily. "I hope so."

"Come"—Dixie took his arm—"let's take Perry out."

So they spent the last hour of the afternoon flying the falcon.

"I've never seen anything that could fly like him," Dixie said.

"There isn't anything that can fly like a peregrine. They're the fastest bird in the air."

Dixie was pleased when Perry came to the gauntlet on her arm. He stood preening his feathers, and she stroked his breast gently. "He's the most beautiful bird I've ever seen."

Then they went back to the mew and brought out the female fledgling.

"Sunlight, you've got to learn to come

back," Jared told her. He placed bait on the ground and let the falcon go to it. Then he tried to entice her back to his gauntlet. About one time in ten, Sunlight would return. "She's still a long ways away from being able to fly free, but we'll keep working on it."

"I'll say in the story how hard it is to train falcons."

Jared suddenly grinned. "You might put something in there about Mrs. McGeltner."

"What about Mrs. McGeltner?"

"If she'd have as much patience with us as we have with this falcon, we might learn more."

Dixie thought hard. "That's a good idea."

"It would be something, wouldn't it, if then Mrs. McGeltner read our story in *Young American?*"

"Oh, I wouldn't use her *name!* I'll just use an imaginary teacher—like Mrs. Smith."

"There are lots of Mrs. Smith teachers out there. You better be careful."

"Oh, don't be silly, Jared!"

"I'm not being silly. People get sued all the time for all kinds of crazy things. If we win that prize, I sure wouldn't want some math teacher named Smith to get it away from us because we insulted him."

They decided to forget the idea.

Back at the house, Dixie played awhile with Dreama. She had become very attached to the baby. And tonight she had permission from her uncle and aunt to make supper for Jared and his father.

The meal consisted of baked pork chops, crispy fried potatoes, green beans with bacon, and applesauce. For dessert, Dixie had made her favorite brownies.

When Jared and Mr. Eagle sat down and Dreama was in her high chair, Dixie said, "I hope you like everything."

"We'd be crazy if we didn't," his father said.

"Will you ask the blessing, Mr. Eagle?"

Jim Eagle right away bowed his head and said a prayer. He must have been thinking a lot about his life lately, Dixie thought. Sometimes he even talked about his wife, which he had not been able to do at first.

Grinning, he said, "Whoever gets you for a wife will have a good cook, Dixie."

After dinner, Jared said, "You did the

cooking, so I'll wash the dishes. You'd better get on home before it gets too dark."

"All right, and I'll see you tomorrow."

"It was a fine meal, Dixie."

After Dixie left, Jared washed the dishes, and his father insisted on helping. His dad said, "I used to help your mother like this. Do you remember?"

"Sure. You always argued that it wasn't a man's place to do dishes, but you always helped, anyway."

"I liked to tease her." He looked up from the dish he was drying. "Do you miss her a great deal, Jared?"

"Well, sure, Dad. Maybe not as much as I used to . . ."

"What would you think if I married again?"

Jared looked at his father and said, "Are you talking about Miss Sarah?"

"She's a fine lady, but I'm not sure she'd marry me."

"Because we're Indian?"

"I don't think that matters to her," his father said thoughtfully. "No, I don't think that's why she might turn me down."

"Why, then?"

"Because it's asking a lot for a young lady to take on a ready-made family."

"But she likes Dreama. And I guess she likes me OK." He faced his father squarely. "Are you going to ask her?"

"I wanted to see how you felt about it first. I wouldn't want to do anything to hurt you, son."

"It wouldn't hurt me. I like Miss Sarah all right. It would be nice to have a mother around the house. I wouldn't have to do dishes then."

"You hooligan!" Jim Eagle grinned and yanked his son's hair.

"Just kidding, Dad. Really. It would be great for Dreama to have a mother. You and me, we do the best we can, but we're not the same thing as a mom."

His dad nodded. Jared thought his face was fixed as if he had decided something.

"I'll have to pray more about it," he said. "I don't have judgment enough to make this kind of decision by myself."

"That's one good thing she's done for you—Miss Sarah, I mean. She's got you to go to church again. You're like you used to be before Mom died. Remember how you liked church then?"

"Miss Sarah's helped me get a lot of things sorted out with God. Anyway, I won't be asking her tonight. Why don't you get out the Monopoly board, and I'll beat you again."

"You haven't beat me in the last five games!" Jared grinned. Then he went to get the game.

Dixie felt Jared squirming uncomfortably in the church pew beside her. He was looking down at his hands. They were tightly clenched.

"What's wrong, Jared? Are you sick?" she whispered.

"No."

The word came out shortly, and he did not look at her. He had seemed all right in Sunday school class. He had even volunteered a few of his thoughts to their teacher. He had been all right during the song service. But when Pastor Stone was halfway through his sermon, Dixie noticed that Jared was behaving most peculiarly.

She thought hard, trying to think what was the matter. *Doesn't he like the sermon?* she thought. It was on "You must be born again." Dixie had heard sermons like it many times. She saw that Jared's coppery skin was a little pale. He must not be feeling well.

Jared could not have told Dixie what was wrong if he had wanted to. Capitan had seemed better this morning, and that had encouraged him. He and his dad had dressed Dreama in a new dress and brought her to church. He had enjoyed the Sunday school class. And the singing. He liked to hear his dad sing, and he liked to sing himself.

Jared had the habit of sometimes drifting off in thought. And when the sermon began, he started thinking about Capitan. He listened to the sermon with one part of his mind and with the other part he was wondering about his horse. He decided to pray. *God, make Capitan get well. Please.*

And suddenly something strange happened. He was hearing what the pastor was saying as clearly as the sound of a trumpet.

"Unless one is born again, he cannot see the kingdom of God!" Pastor Stone said. "No matter how many times you join a church, that won't get you to heaven. No matter how good you try to be, that won't get you to heaven. Only one thing lets any of us come to God, and that is the blood of His Son, Jesus Christ."

Jared had heard such words before, but they had not touched him. Brother Stone was saying that those who did not trust Jesus would be separated from God forever. He had heard that before, too, but the thought had not worried him—until now. That was when his hands had begun to tremble, and he clenched them tightly together. He knew that Dixie was watching, but when she asked what was wrong, he just shook his head.

The sermon went on. Now Pastor Stone spoke of how to be saved. "Whoever will call on the name of the Lord will be saved."

The Bible verse seemed to be carved in brass and put before Jared's eyes. The fear that had come over him grew even worse.

Now the pastor was saying, "After you are God's child, you will follow Jesus, but the first step is to confess that you are a sinner. Then all it takes is one call. The dying thief on the cross said just one thing, 'Jesus, remember me when You come in Your kingdom.' But that one sentence made the difference between dying lost—forever cut off from God—and dying saved and going to be with Jesus."

Finally the end of the sermon came. "You have now heard the gospel. Will *you* admit that you have done wrong? Second, will *you* call upon God, asking Him to forgive your sins for Jesus' sake? If you will do these two things, you, like that thief on the cross, will someday be in heaven."

All the people bowed their heads, and Pastor Stone prayed for those who needed to make decisions.

Jared knew he had to do something.

He began to pray silently, *God, I've done so many bad things. I'm sorry for them all. I wish I hadn't done them, but I just can't seem to help myself. The preacher says I have to tell You that I'm a sinner. Well, I am, Lord. And he says that I have to call upon You to save me. So, right now, I ask You to forgive me for Jesus' sake.*

As soon as Pastor Stone closed his prayer, he said, "We will now stand and sing a hymn. If you have just now trusted Jesus Christ as your Savior, I invite you to come and make your decision public."

The choir and the congregation began to sing.

"Dixie—will you go up with me? I'm afraid."

Dixie was amazed. But she took one look at Jared's face and said, "Sure. I'll go with you."

She took his hand, and they stepped into the aisle. She saw that Jared's father was watching with approval. Aunt Sarah was smiling.

Pastor Stone asked them to sit on the front seat. He knelt down so that he would be Jared's height, and he said, "Jared, has the Lord been speaking to you about your sin?" When Jared nodded, the pastor said, "Have you asked the Lord to forgive your sins because Jesus died for you?"

Jared said, "Yes. I did that, preacher."

"Then let's just pray one more time and thank God that you're now in the family of God."

After the service, nearly everybody in the congregation walked up to shake hands with Jared. Dixie stood beside him, and she shook hands with them, too. Even Billy Joe Satterfield came by. He whispered, "I thought you would tell on me, but you didn't. I'm never going to forget you for that."

\* \* \*

It was a great day for Jim Eagle and his son. Sarah Logan took them home in triumph, and they had a celebration dinner.

After dinner, Jim Eagle asked Sarah to come outside for a walk. As soon as they were under the pecan trees where the wind was blowing softly, he said, "I want to thank you, Sarah."

"For what?"

"For a lot of things. I was pretty far down when I met you, but I've come back to God now. I'll be going back to engineering pretty soon. I think Jared's decision to trust Christ—well, you had a part in that."

"That was mostly Dixie," she said, "but I'm grateful if I was a help."

"I want to ask you . . ."

Sarah waited.

But he shook his head. "Some other time."

Sarah seemed disappointed, but she said, "All right, Jim. Anytime you want to talk, I'll be ready."

# 12

# EL CAPITAN

In every school in the world, perhaps, there are the "ins" and the "outs." Usually a small group will be "in," and they will get chosen for all the important offices. This little group will look down on everyone else as being less important. Usually there is a struggle on the part of the "outs" to get in, but the "ins" try to keep the "outs" out.

In Milo Middle School the leader of the "ins" was Francine Mosely. Dixie had never been invited into this group and would not have joined even if she had been invited. She had strong memories of how terribly Francine had treated Manny Romanos. She had even accused him of stealing her horse.

It seemed Francine always had to find somebody to find fault with, and her latest victim was Jared Eagle. She never missed an opportunity to make fun of him, and her friends joined right in. She even got some of them to do a little war dance every time Jared went by.

Francine's second in command was Billy Joe Satterfield. One thing you could always count on, Dixie well knew, was that Billy Joe Satterfield would always side with Francine Mosely, no matter what she said or did.

English class started as usual with Mrs. McGeltner checking attendance. Then she plunged into a discussion of fiction. The book she had chosen to talk about was *The Last of the Mohicans.* The class has been reading it for two weeks.

Mrs. McGeltner looked about the room. "What do we learn about life from reading *The Last of the Mohicans,* class?"

"I know, Mrs. McGeltner," Francine Mosely said.

As soon as Dixie heard her voice, she glanced across the aisle and saw the secret smile on the girl's face. Dixie's heart sank.

Mrs. McGeltner smiled sweetly. "And what do you think the book is about, Francine?"

"It teaches us that we have to be careful about people who aren't real Americans."

Instantly an alarm went off in Dixie's head. *She's going to make fun of Indians,* she thought. She shot an agonized glance at Jared.

His lips were drawn into a white line. He also knew what was coming.

"Whatever do you mean, Francine?" Mrs. McGeltner asked.

"Why, all through the book the author talks about how treacherous the Indians are. So he's saying that we have to learn not to trust people who are different from us."

At this point, Dixie wanted to punch Francine Mosely out. She was about ready to do it, too, but she remembered how disappointed her uncle and aunt had been when she got into a fight in English class before. She bit her lip to keep from speaking and prepared for what Francine would say next.

However, at that minute, Dixie—and probably everyone else in the class—got the biggest surprise she could imagine.

"I don't think you ought to talk like that, Francine!"

Everyone turned around to stare at Billy Joe Satterfield. "Sure, some Indians in the book aren't so hot," he said loudly. "But some of the other people in the book aren't so hot either. You can't judge somebody by what *race* they belong to. You have to judge them as individuals."

And that came from one of Francine's friends!

Dixie's eyes flew open, and her mouth dropped open as well. Jared glanced back at her, and she saw that he was fully as surprised as she was. Then they both turned back to Billy Joe, who was still talking.

He looked at Francine defiantly. "Until you learn a little bit more about people, Francine, you ought to keep your mouth shut!"

Francine looked like a fish pulled out of the water! Her mouth was open, and she was trying to speak but couldn't say anything.

Mrs. McGeltner said quietly, "Billy Joe, I didn't call on you."

"But this time Francine doesn't know what she's talking about! One of the best characters in the book was an Indian. He was a good guy." Billy Joe looked over at

Jared. "I've treated you rotten, and I'm sorry. You won't hear any more out of me." He turned to Francine. "And if you got any sense, you'll keep your mouth shut, too."

After class, Francine shot out of her seat. She was furious. She said to Billy Joe, "You just stay away from me!" She walked out with her nose in the air.

Billy Joe called after her, "Be an easy thing to do!"

Dixie and Jared and Billy Joe walked out of class together.

"That was a wonderful thing you did, Billy Joe," Dixie said softly.

"Don't say anything else," he said. "I was wrong and that's it."

Jared said, "You didn't have to do that, Billy Joe. I appreciate it."

As the three walked on down the hall, Dixie thought that something had certainly changed in Billy Joe Satterfield.

After school, she was certain of it. She and Jared caught up with him out on the sidewalk. He was looking rather lonely, and she said, "What's the matter? Francine snub you?"

"Who cares what she does? I must have been nuts following around after her.

She's just a stuck-up snob." He hesitated, then said, "I—I got to tell somebody about shooting that falcon."

Dixie and Jared just looked at him, not understanding.

"Why?" Jared asked finally.

"I can't sleep, thinking about it. It was a mistake, but I did it. I've got to go tell Sheriff Peck."

Dixie said, "Maybe it *would* be good if you did, Billy Joe. Things like this don't go away—they just get worse. I know, because I've tried to cover up a few things in my life."

"So have I," Jared said unexpectedly. "I'll go with you."

"I'll go, too," Dixie said.

Billy Joe swallowed hard. "I'll probably go to jail."

Billy Joe Satterfield's father stood looking at his son. Sheriff Peck watched him from across his desk. Dixie and Jared were standing against the wall, saying nothing at all.

Billy Joe looked up at his father. "I'm sorry, Dad, but ever since I shot that falcon, I've felt bad about it. Even if I go to jail, I had to tell."

Mr. Satterfield put his arm around his son's shoulders. "I haven't always been proud of you, Billy Joe, but I'm proud of you today. As a matter of fact, no man could be prouder of his son."

"You mean it?"

"Sure, I mean it. It took courage to turn yourself in. And no matter what happens, I'm with you."

"He won't have to go to jail, will he, Sheriff Peck?" Dixie was unable to keep still.

"No, no, I don't think it will come to that," the sheriff said. He leaned forward, locked his fingers together, and rested them on the desk. "There may be a fine to pay, but I think that's as far as it will go, since the whole thing was unintentional."

"Doesn't matter about the money," Mr. Satterfield said. His eyes were filled with pride. "Just let me know what we need to do."

"Well, I think Billy Joe's in good hands. He's got a good dad and a good mother, and he's got some good friends, and I'm one of them. So we're going to get out of this just fine."

Billy Joe's lower lip trembled. There

was no doubt he had expected to go to jail. "I'll never do anything like that again."

Now Dixie and Jared both went over to him.

Jared punched him on the shoulder. "Why don't you come to my house? I'll show you how to train a falcon."

Dixie added, "I think we ought to go out and have a victory celebration."

Billy Joe looked at them gratefully. "I just lost a lot of friends. Francine and her bunch won't talk to me."

"That's something to be thankful for," Jared grunted. "Let's go to Baskin Robbins and see who can eat a banana split the quickest."

The whole school was amazed at the change in Billy Joe Satterfield. He and Jared became the best of friends. The two boys spent every afternoon after school at the Indian boy's house, working with the falcons.

But the biggest thing that happened the following week had nothing to do with falcons. Dixie was out with her aunt, checking on sick animals at different places. After the last one, Aunt Sarah said,

"Let's run out and see how Capitan is doing."

As they bumped along the country roads in the Cherokee, Dixie said, "Jared's real worried about Capitan."

"I can't figure out anything else to do for that horse," Sarah said, gripping the wheel tightly. "I've done everything I know of. Nothing has worked. I'm still not even sure what's wrong with him."

"I've been praying that he'll get well. You don't think it's wrong to pray for an animal, do you?"

"Certainly not. God is interested in everything we are interested in. That horse means a lot to Jared and his father."

They pulled into the Eagles' yard, and Jared came running, his face alight. Even as they got out of the car, he was hollering, "Miss Sarah, he's better! He's better! Come and see!" He grabbed her by the hand, and they ran to the pasture where Capitan was standing. "Look! You see? Look how bright his eyes are!"

Aunt Sarah stood stock-still. "He does look better," she breathed. Then she went inside the fence and ran her hands over the

157

animal. "He doesn't have any more fever. I can't imagine what's suddenly happened!"

"I don't think it has anything to do with you, Sarah."

Aunt Sarah turned, and there was Mr. Eagle. He put his hand on Jared's shoulder and another on the top fence rail. He was grinning. "I figure it's all the praying that Jared and Dixie have been doing."

Aunt Sarah laughed aloud. "I think you're absolutely right. I've been praying more than a little bit myself."

"So have I." Jim Eagle vaulted over the fence. "Now I want to pay our bill."

"Why, there's no bill. I wouldn't charge you for this trip."

"I wasn't thinking of money."

Before Aunt Sarah could move, Mr. Eagle kissed her on the cheek. "If you want to give me the fee back, I'd be glad to take it," he remarked, still grinning.

Sarah's face grew bright red. She shot a hurried glance at Dixie and Jared, who were both laughing.

Mr. Eagle said, "I never much liked paying out money, but this kind of bill paying I like pretty well."

"You are awful, Jim Eagle!"

"Could be. Come on in the house. Jared and I started supper, and I think we've burned everything. You womenfolk will have to get us out of it."

Aunt Sarah winked at Dixie. She said, "It takes a woman to get a man out of trouble. That's what the Bible says."

"Where does it say that?" Mr. Eagle demanded.

"In the very first book—in Genesis. God took one look at Adam and said, 'Man, you need a helper!'"

# 13

# FREEDOM

I don't see how we can win any prize," Jared said, "and I don't see why a fish doesn't bite this!"

He checked his hook to see if the bait was still there. As usual, Dixie was catching more than he was. Still complaining, he threw his line back.

Even as Jared's cork hit the water, Dixie's disappeared with a *plunk.* She screamed and began pulling. Her line zigzagged around in the creek until finally she brought up a fine red-eared perch.

"That makes twelve for me," she said. "How many have you got?"

Jared scowled. "You must put a spell on those fish. What do you do—spit on your bait?"

Dixie carefully removed the hook and

put the struggling fish into the fish basket. "Let's go home. This is as many as I want to clean."

They gathered their gear and trudged toward Jared's house. He went back to talking about the contest. "We might as well give up on my saddle and your Belize trip."

"Never give up," Dixie said stubbornly.

"You know it's not going to work. We're not going to win the prize. But that's OK. I'm just glad Capitan's OK. I don't care if I have to use a feed sack for a saddle."

Dixie smiled. "I'm glad you feel that way, but I still think we've got a chance to win."

They crossed the field and went through a hickory thicket. Jared pointed to the squirrels running across a top limb. "You just wait," he warned them. "I'll be back for you later."

They cleaned the fish right away, and Dixie said, "Let's put these in the frig for now. I'll take half of them home to Uncle Roy and Aunt Edith."

Mr. Eagle was holding Dreama when they took the pan of fish inside. "Did you catch anything?"

"Don't we always?" Dixie said. She

held up the pan. "How do you like that for fish?"

"They look good to me. Oh, by the way, Jared, a letter came for you today."

Jared's eyes grew wide.

"It's on the table by the front door."

Jared ran off at once.

Dixie had no sooner gotten the fish into the refrigerator than he came back, yelling, "It's from *Young American!*"

"What does it say?" she cried.

"I haven't opened it yet."

"Well, open it! I can't stand the suspense!"

"What's supposed to be in that letter?" his father asked, putting Dreama down to crawl around on the floor.

"It's that contest I told you about, Dad."

"Oh, yeah. Well, open it up. Let's see what you won."

Jared pulled out the letter, and he and Dixie stood together, staring at it. They both read the words aloud.

Dear Jared and Dixie,
    We are pleased to inform you that you have won first prize . . .

They got no farther than that, for Jared let out a wild scream. He began to jump up and down. Dixie joined in his dance, and Mr. Eagle laughed as the two of them careened around the kitchen.

"You're going to scare the baby!" he complained. "But congratulations, anyway."

It took some time for Dixie and Jared to calm down.

But finally Dixie said, "Now you can get that saddle, and I can go to Belize."

Jared still looked to be in a daze. "I can't believe it," he said. "I guess that shows we ought never to doubt God."

"He's always able to do what needs to be done." Then Dixie said, "Let's go out and fly Perry. It's too early for me to go home."

Out in the fields, Perry rode on Dixie's arm.

"Are you ready?" Jared asked.

"Sure," said Dixie. She removed the hood from the falcon's eyes and then, with a sweep of her arm, threw him high in the air. "Go! Get something to eat, Perry!"

The falcon began beating the air with his pinions. He soared skyward.

And then Jared said, "Dixie, look at that!"

"What is it?"

"I think it's another peregrine." He peered up into the afternoon sky. "It could be a female."

The two falcons approached each other, and Dixie could clearly hear one of them making a peculiar sound.

"I don't think we'll be seeing him again," Jared said.

"What do you mean?"

"I mean I think he's interested in things besides coming back here. Yep, there they go."

The two falcons, still circling each other and making odd cries, began to fly away. The female peregrine was in the lead, and Perry was following close behind.

"Good-bye, Perry," Jared said sadly.

"I bet you really hate to see him go."

"Yes, but he'll have a lot more fun now that he's loose. Maybe someday we can find his nest and take pictures of some of his fledglings."

When they told his father what had happened, Mr. Eagle said, "Perry will be occupied with his falcon wife now. Are you jealous, Jared?"

"Aw, Dad, you know I'm happy for

Perry. He'll have his own family now and all the freedom he wants."

"Yep, a bird needs that. A man, too."

Later, Aunt Sarah came to pick up Dixie. While the two adults were talking in the kitchen, Jared said, "Let's go do something outside. They don't want us around."

Dixie grinned. "I guess not. What do you want to do?"

"I found a nest over in the big oak tree. Let's climb up and see if there are any eggs in it."

The tree was very old and enormous in size. Fortunately, the lower limbs came down to about ten feet from the ground, so, with the help of a ladder, it was not difficult to get started. They climbed until they reached the branch the nest was on.

"Wow, you can see clear over to the pond from here," Jared said.

"Never mind that. Let's see if there are any eggs."

Dixie crept carefully out onto the limb, followed by Jared on a parallel branch. She looked inside the nest and let out a cry of delight. "There are three of them!" They were sky blue with small white speckles.

Jared leaned over precariously to see.

"Wonder what they are. They're pretty, though."

They stayed up in the tree for some time, just looking around, and then began their descent. They had almost reached the lowest branches when Dixie said, "Who's that coming?"

Both stopped where they were, and Jared said, "It's Dad and Dreama—and your aunt. Looks like they're headed right for this tree."

"*Sh!* Maybe we can listen to them."

"That's eavesdropping!" Jared said indignantly.

"Well, don't you want to hear?"

Grinning impudently, Jared nodded. "I guess so."

Mr. Eagle and Aunt Sarah stopped under the oak tree. They must have been talking about Jared, for his father said, "He's as good a son as I'd ever hoped to have."

"He's a fine boy," Aunt Sarah agreed. "You couldn't ask for a better son. And Dreama here—she's just a doll."

Then Mr. Eagle said, "I started to ask you a question once, Sarah, but I couldn't get up the nerve. I guess you know what the question is. I want you to marry me. Will you? I know it's hard for a woman to accept a ready-made family . . ."

"If a woman loves a man, she'll love his children too," Aunt Sarah said softly.

"Does that mean that you *will* marry me?"

"I just don't know if Jared will accept another woman as his mother."

At that moment Dixie, who had been leaning over to listen, suddenly lost her grip. She let out a yelp. "I'm falling!" She slipped down to the next limb and hung there like ripe fruit. "Help!"

"Just drop, Dixie!" Jared's father called. "I'll catch you!"

"Ow, I'm falling!"

Dixie fell, but she was caught in Mr. Eagle's strong arms.

Jared scrambled down the tree. He went right to Dixie's aunt and smiled up at her. "You can be my mom if you want to," he said.

"You were listening!" Aunt Sarah cried.

"Well, if you two are gonna roam out in the open, you ought to look up in the trees!" Jared's grin was even wider.

Aunt Sarah burst out laughing and put

her arms around him. "I'd love to be your mom, Jared."

"You would?" Mr. Eagle said. He looked down at Dreama. "And what about her?"

Aunt Sarah said, "I'm the luckiest girl in the world to get a handsome husband and two fine kids like this all at one time."

Dixie yelled, "Hooray! Can I be your bridesmaid?"

Jared pulled her hair. "You always want to be the star."

"Ow!" Dixie got a handful of Jared's hair before they fell to the ground and went rolling over and over until his dad separated them. "You two ought to act nicer."

"He started it!" Dixie said.

Jared grinned. "I'll be in the wedding, too, won't I, Mom?"

Aunt Sarah's eyes seemed full of diamonds. "You can be in my wedding anytime. Let's go inside and make big plans."

And then they all trooped toward the house. Dixie Morris suspected that her Aunt Sarah was going to be very busy in the days to come.